CHARM CITY

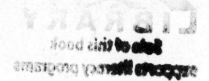

Visit us at www.boldstrokesbooks.com

By the Author

By Mason Dixon

Date With Destiny

Charm City

By Yolanda Wallace

In Medias Res

Rum Spring

Lucky Loser

Month of Sundays

Murphy's Law

The War Within

CHARM CITY

by

Mason Dixon

2014

CHARM CITY

ISBN 13: 978-1-62639-198-7

THIS TRADE PAPERBACK ORIGINAL IS PUBLISHED BY
BOLD STROKES BOOKS, INC.
P.O. BOX 249
VALLEY FALLS, NY 12185

FIRST EDITION: AUGUST 2014

CREDITS
EDITOR: CINDY CRESAP
PRODUCTION DESIGN: SUSAN RAMUNDO
COVER DESIGN BY SHERI (GRAPHICARTIST2020@HOTMAIL.COM)

Acknowledgments

Life is composed of a series of choices. Some good, some bad. Some easy, some difficult. The characters in *Charm City* have made some tough choices and are trying to live with the results.

My decision to adopt the Mason Dixon pen name was a tough one as well—I get a thrill each time I see my name on the spine of a book I've written—but the results of the move, including a Lambda Literary Award nomination for Mason's first book *Date With Destiny*, have been much better than I expected.

Mason's books will continue to feature women of color as the main characters, and I hope they will continue to reach an audience. I don't write because I want to make a political statement. I write because I have stories to tell. Stories that feature fictional characters as diverse as the ones readers encounter in real life. Love is love, no matter the ethnic background of those feeling its effects.

Thank you to Radclyffe and the rest of the BSB team for allowing me to create my stories using all the colors in the rainbow.

Yolanda "Mason Dixon" Wallace

Dedication

To my boo. Thanks for always having my back.

CHAPTER ONE

R aq knew her hand was broken even before she heard the bones snap.

Ice had said her opponent—a five-foot-nothing Asian chick who had lots of speed but very little power—had a glass jaw. But when Raq landed a hook that left her hand looking like she had a bag of rocks under her skin, the shit felt like reinforced steel.

The Asian chick went down from the blow and stayed down for the count. That was no big surprise. Ice didn't believe in weight classes, so Raq outweighed her opponent by a good thirty pounds. As soon as she tapped her once, Raq knew it would be lights out. But even though her opponent lost the fight, she put Raq out of commission for two months. Eight weeks without a bout had put a serious hurt on Raq's pocketbook.

Ice had offered her some other jobs so she could make some paper while she healed up, but those gigs didn't pay nearly as much as her primary one or earn the same amount of respect on the streets. Not the gigs she was willing to accept, anyway. For her, the underground fights she participated in were a way of life. For Ice, they were nothing more than a nice sideline. The icing on an already sweet cake. She knew how he made his real money, but she didn't get down like that. Never had. Never would.

Today was her first day back in the gym since the uptight nurse at the free clinic cut off her cast with a tiny saw she had allowed to drift a little too close to Raq's skin. Raq flexed her fingers as she tested the tape on her hands. Her right hand felt pretty good, but the left was a little tight. The hand was already swollen, and she hadn't even thrown the first punch.

"What up, Raq?"

"Wassup, Zeke?" she asked, giving him a pound.

Zeke Walker's build was slight, but his voice was deep. Just like his father. When he said, "Same old, same old," he sounded just like the old man.

The sign outside the run-down building read Pop's Gym. Ezekiel "Pop" Walker Sr. had been retired for five years now. His son, Ezekiel Jr., had taken over the business, but he hadn't inherited the name. Not all of it, anyway.

"You ready to do this?" Zeke asked.

"Ready and willing."

"After you warm up on the jump rope, I'll work with you on the heavy bag. Then you can finish up with some speed work on your own."

"What about sparring? There must be someone here who needs some ring work today."

"Plenty, but I don't want you to take too much of a chance on that hand on your first day back. I don't want Ice to come after me if I let his moneymaker get hurt."

Raq looked longingly toward the ring, where two male heavyweights in thickly padded protective gear were doing more clinching than punching. She had never fought against a man for pay, but she had sparred with several of them before. She had held her own each time out. She had even knocked one down with a right hook he hadn't seen coming. He had tried to play it off like he had slipped on a wet spot on the canvas, but she could tell by the glazed look in his eyes her punch was the real reason he had ended up on his ass.

She wished Ice would set up a bout for her against a guy—especially one of those cocksure hotshots who thought they were all that because they'd managed to get in a lucky punch a time or two—but he kept saying "the streets weren't ready." More like the odds weren't long enough for him to turn a suitable profit. When the money was right, maybe she'd finally get her shot.

"You know where everything is," Zeke said, pulling her out of fantasyland. "I'll come back in half an hour and spot you on the heavy bag. Cool?"

"Cool."

She gave him another pound and picked up a worn jump rope with heavy wooden handles. The wood had been worn smooth over time, and the once-white rope had faded to a dusky gray.

Raq flicked her wrists, whipping the rope over her head and down toward her feet. Her heart rate rose as she quickly found her rhythm. She used to hate training, but she hadn't realized how much she'd missed it. The sound of the rope whipping through the air and slapping on the scuffed floor beneath her bouncing feet. The smell of sweat, blood, and spit buckets. The sense of belonging.

Pop's wasn't one of those upscale places where yuppies spent their lunch hours working out in designer wind suits and two-hundred-dollar tennis shoes. It was the kind of place frequented by plain folks in sweatpants, ratty tank tops, and run-over boxing shoes with soles as thin as a sheet of notebook paper. It was the kind of place where desperate people tried to buy a ticket out of the 'hood.

No one came to Pop's because they wanted to. They came because they had to. They came because they had nowhere else to go. They came because Pop's offered their best chance to make a name for themselves on something other than a police blotter. They came because this was the only place that would allow them to put their pictures alongside Jack Johnson, Sugar Ray Robinson, Muhammad Ali, Marvin Hagler, Sugar Ray Leonard, Tommy Hearns, and Mike Tyson on Pop Walker's Wall of Fame. They came because the only people who believed they could be anything but crime statistics were a skinny old man and his son.

Raq felt sweat roll down the intricate tracks of her cornrows and soak into the thin cotton of her wife-beater. She felt something else, too. The electric heat of someone's eyes on her. She scanned the faces on display in the floor-to-ceiling mirror on the opposite wall until she locked eyes with the only other woman in the place.

The woman was pounding the hell out of the speed bag—both the bag and her hands were moving so fast they were nothing but blurs—but her eyes were focused not on the bag but Raq's face. Her eyes were nearly the same shade as her skin, a rich dark brown. Her black hair was pulled back into a ponytail that bounced between her shoulder blades as she moved. Her workout gear was loose fitting, but Raq could tell she had a banging body beneath the baggy clothes. Despite her sharply defined muscles, she projected an air of femininity. The perfect blend of hard and soft.

Raq was twenty-six. The woman appeared to be a year or two older. Her age might have been a mystery, but one thing was certain: she didn't look like any of the women from around here. She didn't look like the kind who would go in for a quick fuck and wouldn't expect or ask Raq to call in the morning. She probably had to be wined and dined before she gave it up. Raq was down for that. As good as the woman looked, she was down for whatever.

Raq squared her shoulders, gave the woman the nod, and mouthed, "Wassup?"

The woman laughed and shook her head as if Raq needed to step up her game.

"Wipe the makeup off your face," Zeke said as he helped her slip on a pair of boxing gloves, "because you just got clowned."

"Who is she, anyway?"

Raq pounded her fists against each other to check the gloves' fit, then dug a right into the heavy bag before following up with a tentative left. The jab didn't have much pop on it, but her hand began to throb nevertheless. She pulled back even more, not wanting to risk re-aggravating her injury. Zeke wasn't the only person Ice would come after if she hurt herself today.

"Bathsheba Morris." Zeke leaned his shoulder into the bag to absorb the blows. The stocking cap he wore to maintain the waves in his closely cropped hair made him look like he had a giant condom on his head, but it got the job done. "She's been coming in three times a week for the past month or so. She hasn't been in the ring yet, but if she's as good in there as she is on the speed bag, she might give you a run for your money."

Raq doubted that. She had yet to meet a woman who could challenge her in the ring or out. Before she busted her hand, Ice had said he was tempted to have her fight two at a time to see if the matches would last longer. She would have been down for that and still might be if it meant she got to take home twice the pay at the end of the night.

"Bathsheba? She must have one of those mamas that prays all the time."

"Either that or she watched too many Pam Grier movies back in the day."

"Can you blame her? That sister was fine." Raq circled the heavy bag like she was stalking an opponent. "What does Bathsheba do?"

"I don't know. Since you're so full of questions, why don't you ask her some of them?"

"Maybe I will."

Zeke grunted as Raq put all her strength into a right that landed squarely on the bag's duct-taped center. "Damn, girl. You could have broken someone's rib with that punch."

Raq smiled at the comment. Mike Tyson, her idol, would have been proud. Before he turned into the circus act who chewed on Evander Holyfield's ears and guest starred in *Hangover* films, he had been the man who had tried to shove Jesse Ferguson's nose bone into his brain.

Raq performed a left-right, left-right combination and turned to see if Bathsheba approved of her show of strength, but a wiry Mexican featherweight was working the speed bag Bathsheba had been using only minutes before. Raq saw her heading for the women's locker room. Just before she turned the corner, Bathsheba stopped and looked over her shoulder as if she wanted Raq to follow her.

"Hell, yeah. That's what's up. I'll be back in a minute, Z." Raq loosened her gloves with her teeth and quickly pulled them off. "I need to take a piss."

"Yeah. Uh huh."

She could tell by his tone he knew she was lying, but if anyone would understand, he would. She would bet serious money none of the guys who trained at Pop's knew Zeke was gay, but she had seen him hugged up on the drag queens at Club Peaches enough times to know he didn't frequent the place for the overpriced drinks.

When Raq got to the women's locker room, which was more of a closet than an actual room, Bathsheba had already unwrapped the bright pink protective bandages on her hands and pulled on a dry sweatshirt over her damp T-shirt. Like Raq, she probably didn't feel safe taking a shower in a facility filled with a bunch of testosterone-filled guys with impulse control issues.

Raq leaned against one of the dented metal lockers Pop had snatched up after one of the local schools shut its doors for lack of funding or lack of interest. Around here, it was hard to tell.

"I saw you on the speed bag. You got some pretty fast hands. What else can they do?"

Bathsheba smiled and shook her head like she had in the gym. "Is that really the best you can do?" she asked, tossing her duffel bag over her shoulder.

Raq shrugged. "This isn't the kind of thing I normally do."

"So you don't go around trying to pick up strange women in gyms every day?"

"No, just three times a week. Isn't that how often you come in?"

Bathsheba flashed a glimmer of a smile. Raq was an expert at reading people's body language. She usually smelled fear when she bore down on someone in the ring. Now, all she could sense was interest.

"Have you been watching me or something?" Bathsheba asked.

"I don't have to. I have people everywhere."

"I'll watch my back from now on."

"I'd rather watch your front."

Bathsheba groaned and rolled her eyes. "That was your worst one yet."

"That's 'cause I was trying to make you smile. See? It worked." Raq took a step closer. "I'm Raq."

"Oh, I know exactly who you are." Bathsheba folded her arms in front of her chest, framing a pair of nicely sized breasts. Raq licked her lips as she imagined getting a taste of them.

"Then why don't I know you?"

"You and your people must not have been paying attention because I've been right here the whole time."

"Let me make up for that mistake."

"How?"

Raq moved closer still, but Bathsheba didn't give ground. During a fight, Raq liked to crowd her opponents into a corner and wale on them until they went down or their seconds threw in the towel. Bathsheba probably tried to keep the action in the center of the ring, where speed mattered more than power.

"Let me take you out for a drink or a bite to eat. Can I get your number?"

"No."

"Why not?"

"Because I don't give away things that need to be earned." Bathsheba spread her arms and indicated the body Raq had been ogling all afternoon. "You have to earn this."

"Don't worry," Raq said after Bathsheba stepped around her and began to walk away. "I intend to."

❖

Bathsheba's hands shook as she sat behind the wheel of her car. She had campaigned for this assignment because she thought she was most qualified to take it on. The other officers in Major Crimes knew the streets of the Middle East as well as she did, if not better, but their faces were so visible in the rundown area infamous for its rampant crime and numerous abandoned houses, the people they wanted to take down knew exactly who they were and where to find them.

She had grown up in this neighborhood. Come of age here. But she had gotten out when she was sixteen. After ten years in DC, where she was known by her middle name instead of her first, she was back.

Isaac "Ice" Taylor had been running the streets of East Baltimore for almost eight years, quite an accomplishment for a man still on the right side of thirty. He owned several legal businesses ranging from a real estate agency to the soul food restaurant that served as his headquarters, but his illegal empire was even more vast—drugs, prostitution, and illegal gambling on everything from dogfights to underground bareknuckle boxing matches.

Everyone knew what Ice Taylor was up to, but the cops had never been able to pin anything on him that the DA's office could get to stick. Witnesses either clammed up or disappeared.

Associates, despite generous plea deals or offers of immunity, refused to roll over. Because no one crossed Ice Taylor.

After months of lobbying, Bathsheba had finally been able to convince her superiors in the newly formed Middle Eastern Division what they already knew: the only way to bring Taylor down was from the inside. Thanks to Raquel Overstreet, Ice's favorite enforcer and the best, most punishing boxer in his ever-growing stable, Bathsheba had just found her way in.

Bathsheba thought of the videos she had seen uploaded to the Internet. She had studied the shaky images almost daily while she prepared herself for this assignment. The merciless woman she had watched mow down overmatched opponents in makeshift rings in backyards, abandoned warehouses, and back alleys was nothing like the woman she had met today.

The woman she had encountered in Pop's Gym had an unexpected sweetness about her. An undeniable appeal. If she didn't know what Raq did for a living or who she worked for, Bathsheba wouldn't mind getting to know her better.

Bathsheba stared at her reflection in the rearview mirror. When an officer went undercover, she had to completely commit herself to the role she was assigned to play in order to lessen the risk of discovery and increase the chance of success. Ice Taylor had been ruling the streets of the Middle East for far too long. How far was she willing to go to get her man?

"As far as it takes," she said, feeling her jangled nerves begin to steady. "As far as it takes."

CHAPTER TWO

R aq wished she had worn gloves. She rubbed her hands together to ward off the cold. October wasn't normally this bad. Or maybe she simply wasn't used to standing on street corners babysitting junior gangsters all day. Half Pint sold more product than anyone in Ice's crew, but he probably didn't know how to wipe his own ass, let alone cover it.

"Five-oh," she called out as she saw a patrolling police car turn the corner at the end of the block. She pushed off the wall she was leaning against, shoved her hands in the pockets of her low-slung jeans, and hardened her expression as the car began to roll up.

Half Pint pulled ten small plastic-wrapped packages from his pocket and dropped them at his feet. Then he covered them with a piece of cardboard that had been laid there for that purpose. The packets wouldn't be hard to find if the cops looked hard enough, but since the baggies weren't on Half Pint, he couldn't be charged with possession.

The police car slowed as it passed by. The beefy, red-faced cop taking up most of the passenger's seat stuck his head out the window. "Pull your pants up."

Like most guys Raq knew, Half Pint's pants started out well south of his ass and the hems pooled around his

Timberland boots. A good eight inches of plaid cotton peeked between his belt and the bottom of his Ray Lewis jersey. Hers were only slightly higher, but the cop wasn't looking at her. His eyes were squarely on Half Pint.

"Have a good day, Officer." Half Pint held two fingers against the flat bill of his side-turned baseball cap. As soon as the police car was far enough away, he turned the salute into a middle-fingered one. "Fucking pigs." He bent to pick up the drugs he had dropped. "Why can't they leave me alone and let me do my job, man?"

"They have a job to do, too. If they don't meet their quotas, it comes out of their budget."

Half Pint sucked air through his teeth in disapproval. "If I don't meet mine, it comes out of my ass. When it comes to his money, Ice don't play."

"True that." Raq held out her fist and gave him a pound. Then she lifted her Terps cap to scratch her head. Her cornrows were getting loose and she needed to get them redone, but she didn't have the scratch. Not many people braided hair for free. The ones who did were lousy at it, plus Raq would have to hit them up first. Too bad they were usually lousy at that, too. "Heads up."

One of Half Pint's most persistent customers was lurching toward them, scratching at her face and arms as if she had something crawling on her skin. Everyone called her Gumby because she didn't have any teeth, but her real name was Deborah or Delilah or some shit. Something that started with a D.

"Looks like someone needs a fix," Half Pint said, lighting up one of the singles he had bought from the corner store.

Raq took in Gumby's outfit. She was wearing a dirty sweater, ragged jeans, and a pair of men's house shoes that were at least two sizes too big. "Does she have money?"

Half Pint blew out a stream of cigarette smoke. "She don't need it."

"Since when? You giving freebies now?"

"Don't worry, Raq. I got this."

Raq hung back and waited for him to prove it. He had been trying to prove something to one person or another since he'd started out on these streets. His real name was Rashad Jefferson, but everyone called him Half Pint because he was small for his age. He had the Little Man complex to match. He considered the gun he carried in the folds of his jeans his great equalizer, but it was Raq's job to make sure he didn't have to use it.

"You holding, Half Pint?" Gumby asked. She smelled like a skunk that had been rolling around in cigarette butts and malt liquor. And that was just her breath. Raq didn't even want to get started on her body odor.

"I might be."

"Let me get a dime bag," Gumby said.

"You got the cash?" Half Pint asked.

"You know I'm good for it."

"If you're looking for a loan, you need to head to the bank. I don't give something for nothing."

Gumby grabbed the drooping crotch of Half Pint's oversized jeans. "I'll do you right. You know I will."

A grin creased Half Pint's face, making him look even younger than he already was. "All right then. Give me five minutes and I'll meet you in the usual spot."

"Can I get the stuff first?"

Half Pint shook his head. "You know it don't work like that." He pointed to the boarded-up building across the street that had been marked for demolition for so long Raq had forgotten what it used to be. "I'll meet you there in five minutes."

"That's nasty, man," Raq said after Gumby lurched across the street. "Are you really going to hit that?"

"Hell, no, but I'll let her suck me off."

"So you're going to front her ten dollars in exchange for a blow job?"

"The pros would charge me more than that and most of them have all their teeth." He swiveled his narrow hips. "I like the way she gums my shit. Nothing ruins a good blowjob like teeth scraping on my joint. Watch the spot, okay? I'll be back in ten minutes."

"Are you really going to do this shit on company time?"

"Consider this my lunch break. Everyone's entitled to one. I read that someplace. You know where the extra stash is, right?"

"Yeah, but I'm not going to sell any of it for you. That's your deal, man, not mine."

Half Pint frowned like the little boy he was trying not to be. "Slinging crack is a hell of a lot easier than getting punched in the face. I don't know why you pretend you don't want to switch." He put two fingers in his mouth and whistled to get the attention of his partner on the opposite corner. Then he held up his hands to let Little Tony know how long he'd be gone. Little Tony normally acted as a lookout, but he knew how to make a sale if a buyer came along.

Raq moved closer to him so she could cover his back if she needed to. She watched cars come and go, some stopping so their owners could make a buy, others slowing to check out the competition. None of the established dealers were stupid enough to encroach on Ice's turf, but you never knew when some young buck would decide it was his time to try to move up the food chain.

Raq stiffened when a black SUV with tinted windows squealed to a stop a few feet from her position. She searched for a potential escape route when the power window on the passenger's side began to slide down.

"Yo, Raq!"

She relaxed when Desmond Lassiter, Ice's second-in-command, stuck his head out the window. The diamond studs in his ears glittered in the sun. A similarly encrusted cross dangled from a white gold chain around his neck. "Wassup, Dez?" She moved closer to the car. "Sweet ride. When did you get it?"

"I picked it up this morning, but I have to get a new set of rims before I start claiming it as mine. Right now, it looks like something my mama would drive." He stroked his neatly trimmed goatee. His hair was worn in an Afro Raq thought of as his nappy natural. It was always the light-skinned brothers who felt the need to prove how black they were. Dez was no different. "Hop in the back. Ice wants to see you."

Those words always put a chill in Raq's heart. Because, more often than not, they were the last words some people ever heard.

"I can't go anywhere right now. I have to watch the spot until Half Pint gets his rocks off."

"That should take all of two minutes if the chick he's banging can even find what he's working with. Get in. Bigfoot will keep an eye on things until you get back."

The rear door opened and Bigfoot, a six-foot-eight giant who had been an offensive lineman for the Terps before he tore up his knee and flunked out of college, climbed out with a great deal of effort.

"What's good, Raq?" he wheezed.

"Nothing to it, big man."

His playing weight at the University of Maryland had been around three hundred pounds. He had gained a good fifty more since he left school. He couldn't run if you paid him, but once he got his hands on you, you weren't going anywhere until he decided to let you go.

Raq climbed into the backseat of the car and Rico, Dez's driver, pulled away from the curb. Everything about the car smelled new. Like money. Her hand slid over the black leather seats. She looked up to find Dez staring at her. His wide grin made him look like a crocodile.

"It's nice, right?"

"Yeah, it is."

"It's just like me: big, black, and powerful."

He was always fishing for compliments about the size of his dick or his intellect, but Raq had her doubts about both. Besides, she was hired to handle security, not kiss ass.

"Why does Ice want to see me?"

"You know he keeps everything on a need to know basis. And if I don't need to know, I don't want to know. Whatever he wants to talk about is between you and him. The two of you can have an A and B conversation. I will C my way out of it." He pointed to the radio when the new joint from Kanye West began to play. "Yo, turn that up, man. That's my jam right there."

Rico spun the dial until Raq could feel the bass thumping like a heartbeat. Her eardrums were vibrating so much she couldn't keep up with Kanye's tongue-twisting flow. She watched out the darkened windows as the boarded up and knocked out windows of the Middle East's abandoned buildings gave way to the shiny glass and steel of corporate offices and luxury apartments in downtown Baltimore.

Raq always felt out of place here. Even though it was the same city, this part of town didn't feel like her Baltimore.

Her Baltimore consisted of a few blocks bordered by East Biddle Street on the north, East Fayette Street on the south, Bradford Street on the east, and North Broadway on the west. This wasn't her neighborhood. This 'hood belonged to the people who called the shots, not the soldiers who took the orders.

Rico pulled to a stop in front of an apartment building overlooking the Inner Harbor. Several Ravens and Orioles players owned property in the area. Raq had seen them behind the wheels of their six-figure sports cars from time to time. What she wouldn't give to drive one of those babies for an hour, let alone every day.

Dez suddenly spun in his seat, making Raq's heart skip a beat she couldn't afford to lose. "Ice is expecting you. You can handle it from here, can't you? I need to pick up my rims before the shop closes."

"Yeah, I can handle it."

Raq climbed out of the car on shaky legs. She had been to see Ice a thousand times, but the fear never abated. Ice could have anything he wanted at the snap of a finger. Whether it be ordering a plate of blue crabs from one of those restaurants with white tablecloths and formally attired waiters or ordering someone's execution. What did he want with her? She hoped it was something good, but she had to be prepared in case it was something bad.

The doorman outside let her in the building and buzzed her upstairs. Raq rode the glass elevator to the penthouse floor, enjoying the view of the waterfront the whole way. No one she knew lived like this. No one except Ice.

When she approached Ice's apartment, one of his four bodyguards was standing outside the door. Raq didn't know why Ice felt he needed so much protection here. Yes, he was vulnerable on the streets of the Middle East, but who could touch him here? No one, that's who.

Hercules opened the door without offering a greeting. Raq stepped into the foyer and submitted to a pat down, even though everyone knew she never carried.

"You're not being paranoid if they're really out to get you, right?" Ice asked as he refilled his highball glass with Scotch. Raq couldn't stomach the stuff, but Ice swore by it. Probably because the brand he favored cost three figures a bottle. Raq couldn't understand the appeal. Olde English got you just as high for a fraction of the price.

Ice's parents were from a small island in the Caribbean. Bermuda or the Bahamas. Something that started with a B. He had his parents' work ethic, but not their accent. His changed based on his audience. When he addressed his street soldiers, he sounded like someone who was born and raised in the Middle East. When he spoke with Baltimore's officials, policy makers, and moneymen, he sounded like someone from the Ivy League. And when he pulled in one of the string of honeys lining up to take a turn in his bed, he could have passed for Denzel Washington.

Raq envied his versatility—and his money. She wanted to be him when she grew up. Shit. Who didn't?

She looked around the apartment filled with the trappings of wealth. Filled with things she could dream about but would never have.

"Have a seat," Ice said, indicating the chair next to his. "It's almost halftime."

On the fifty-five-inch flat-screen TV, the Ravens were trailing Peyton Manning and the Broncos by a touchdown.

"The defense got ripped to shreds when my man Ray Lewis retired and Ed Reed took the free agent route out of town, but as long as we have Ray Rice carrying the rock and Joe Flacco slinging it, we have a fighting chance, right?"

Raq wanted to tell him it didn't matter how many points the offense put on the board if the defense couldn't stop the other team from scoring, but she didn't want to end up on his bad side for contradicting him.

"Speaking of fights, do you have one for me?"

Ice smiled. Unlike his bodyguards, who favored gold and platinum fronts, his teeth were so white they made him look like he had a mouthful of Chiclets. "That depends. How's the hand?"

"Sore, but I don't need a left when I have a right." She tried to keep her eyes from bugging out of her head when a local female rapper who had recently signed a record deal with one of the major labels walked from the bedroom to the kitchen butt-ass naked.

"You remember the Black Dahlia, don't you?" Ice asked as Dahlia fixed herself something to eat. "Her album drops next month. You should come to the release party. I'll make sure Dez gives you an invitation."

"That'd be cool."

Ice leaned back in his chair. His silk shirt was unbuttoned to the waist, revealing his chiseled chest and rippling abs. On her way back to the bedroom, Dahlia stopped to cop herself a feel.

"I'll be with you in a minute, okay, baby?" Ice said in his best Denzel voice. "I've got some business to take care of first."

Dahlia took her apple bottom, double Ds, and plate of food to the bedroom. It was all Raq could do not to watch her go.

"If I got you a fight, can you promise it will last more than one round? I lose money when you knock bitches out in less than thirty seconds."

"You tell me how long you want the fight to last and I'll make it happen."

Ice stared at her with eyes as cold as his name. "You'd better." He reached for an envelope on the glass-topped coffee table and slid it toward her. Raq looked at it but didn't pick it up. She wouldn't until Ice told her it was okay. "I got you a fight on this week's undercard. You've got to work your way back up to headliner. You'll be fighting one of King's girls. You could probably knock her out in one, but I need you to go three. Understand?"

Raq nodded. The longer the fight went, the more bets got laid down. The more money Ice took home, the more she took home. What was so hard to understand about that?

"There's five hundred dollars in there," Ice said as he fingered the envelope. "Consider it an advance. Buy you a new robe or something for your triumphant return to the ring, or take some girl out to dinner. Are you still seeing that big-tittied chick from East Fayette?"

"Nah, that was a short-term thing."

Ice chuckled as he sipped his Scotch. "I hear you. It doesn't pay to let any of them get their hooks into you for long. Not when there's so many more to choose from."

He nodded, indicating she could pick up the envelope. She reached for it and slid it into the pocket of her hoodie. She thought about Bathsheba and wondered if she could spend some of the money on her. She had to convince her to say yes first, but that was only a matter of time.

"Keep up the good work and there'll be more of that to come," Ice said, draining the rest of his glass. "Now if you'll excuse me, I need to take care of some unfinished business in the bedroom."

Raq almost asked how she was supposed to get home—cabs didn't stop for people who looked like her—but she'd been solving her own problems since she was a kid. What was one more?

She took the bus back to the Middle East. Two, in fact. When she finally got back to the one-bedroom efficiency she called home, she lay on her bed and stared at the cracked ceiling, wishing she had a way out.

The code she lived by helped her sleep at night, but she knew it would never make her rich. She wanted to live high on the hog like Ice did, but she wasn't willing to pay the price. That was okay for now, but what was she supposed to do when she could no longer do what she was doing now? What was she supposed to do when someone younger, faster, and stronger came along?

She closed her eyes, feeling like Scarlett O'Hara. She'd worry about the future tomorrow. Tomorrow was another day.

CHAPTER THREE

B athsheba stood on the coffee table, lifted the ceiling tile, and retrieved her laptop from its hiding place. She needed to update her case files while the details were still fresh in her mind.

She lowered the tile into place, climbed off the table, and sat on the ratty plaid couch. Both the sofa and the matching chair had come with the apartment and had probably been handed down from one tenant to another for about twenty years. She didn't want to think about the source of some of the stains on the worn material. The stains added to the authenticity of her cover, so she didn't try too hard to scrub them out, but she felt like taking a shower each time she sat down, five-second rule be damned.

The apartment was small, with only a living room, bedroom, bathroom, and kitchen. The living room—like the rest of the place—was cramped, with just enough space for the table and chairs and a small stand for the miniscule TV, but it was more room than she'd had growing up, and it was all she needed until her job here was done.

Her real place near the gay bars and restaurants of DC's Dupont Circle wasn't much bigger than this one, but it was both miles and worlds away from the Middle East. The place she currently called home was a run-down apartment complex inhabited by people living well below the poverty line. If you could call it living. For some, it was more like surviving.

Sitting on the newspaper sections she had spread across the couch to protect her skin from the various bodily fluids that had made themselves a permanent part of the fabric covering the cushions, she logged on to her laptop and opened a series of files. She knew she was taking a chance by keeping the computer with her when she had left every other part of her life behind, but both it and the files on it were password-protected, so she felt relatively safe. Relatively being the operative word.

Her nerves were so on edge, a bump outside the double-locked door almost made her jump out of her skin until she realized the noise had been caused by a wayward throw from a game of catch taking place in the litter-strewn street. She took a deep breath to get her heart out of her throat.

She kept telling herself to relax, but her mind wouldn't let her. She kept waiting for someone to recognize her. To remember who she once was. To discover who she had become.

She doubted the neighborhood folks that remembered her had followed her progress out of the 'hood. They didn't know about her graduation from the police academy in DC or her life and career there. Their focus didn't go past the bars of the cage in which they had been trapped. One day soon, she hoped to find the key to that cage. When she did, she could unlock the door for good. Or until the next wannabe kingpin came along. As soon as one fell, there was always another waiting to take his place.

"One step at a time."

After she added the details of her most recent round of surveillance to her case notes, she closed the file and accessed another. She stared at the pictures displayed on the screen—a flowchart of Ice Taylor's operations. Ice, naturally, was at the top of the chart. Desmond Lassiter, his second-in-command, was just below him. After that, it got interesting. Bathsheba followed the branches of Ice's criminal family tree, the lieutenants and the street soldiers that reported to them.

The captions under the photographs read like something out of a crazy baby name book. Ice. Dez. Rico. One-Eyed Mike. Hercules. Winky. Bigfoot. Half Pint. Little Tony. Raq.

Bathsheba leaned closer to the screen to get a better look at the picture of Raq, taken either before or after one of the underground boxing matches that had given Ice's favorite enforcer her street cred. In the picture, a black sports bra accentuated Raq's broad shoulders and solid core. Her thickly muscled legs looked like tree trunks, even under loose-fitting basketball shorts that hung just past her knees. Her fists were raised to her chin as if she were posing for a boxing poster. Bathsheba wondered if Raq could have been a professional boxer. The skills were there, and she certainly had the power to go pro. All she needed was the opportunity. Whether by circumstance or design, Raq's opportunity appeared to have been missed.

Bathsheba shut down the computer and closed it with a click.

"This is no time to start getting sentimental," she cautioned herself. "She made her choices. Now she has to live with the consequences."

But a shadow of doubt entered her mind as she returned her computer to its hiding place. Ice was her target, and she wouldn't stop until she took him down, but how many of his crew would end up going down with him? Most were young and impressionable with limited options and next to no resources. They were only doing what they had been ordered to do. Just like she was.

"It isn't your job to worry about what happens after they get arrested. It's your job to make sure they get the chance to find out."

Her assignment could take a few weeks or a few months, depending on how quickly she was able to infiltrate Ice's operation. Meeting Raq was a start. Now she needed to press her advantage without being too obvious about it. Until she got some traction, she felt like she was spinning her wheels.

She needed to move. She needed to do something so she could feel useful. She went for a run to clear her head. She didn't have a particular destination in mind when she left the apartment, but her body must have because it led her right to Pop's. She had already gotten in some cardio work, thanks to the mile-long jog, so she wrapped her hands with some borrowed tape and headed for the speed bag.

The movements were mind-numbing—she could do them with her eyes closed—but the positioning gave her the perfect vantage point. The location of the bag she favored allowed her to see the entire room without having to work too hard, though the burning muscles in her arms and shoulders might beg to differ.

She bounced on the balls of her feet as she kept up a steady rhythm on the punching bag. The air-filled leather bag slapped against her churning fists and the rebound platform. She hadn't trained this hard since she was a rookie at the police academy when she had treated every day as a test to prove she belonged.

The surroundings were different, but not much had changed. Four years later, she was still trying to prove something. Not to everyone else. To herself.

"Wassup, Zeke?"

Raq's voice, a deep alto dripping with a molasses-thick East Baltimore accent, pulled Bathsheba out of her head and forced her to focus. She watched Raq and Zeke Walker slap palms and give each other a one-armed hug.

Zeke didn't appear to be a player in this complex shell game. He allowed Raq to train in his gym, but he seemed to be doing it out of genuine affection rather than loyalty to Ice. None of Ice's other fighters ever trained here. They simply showed up for their fights—spare tires, bad technique, lack of endurance, and all. But Raq was different. She trained like she was fighting for a purse worth millions instead of a few hundred dollars.

Bathsheba suspected she was fighting for something even more valuable than money: respect.

Raq, who was wearing the same outfit Bathsheba had seen her in the day before—a white tank top and a pair of cut-off heather gray sweatpants—quickly made her way over to her. Bathsheba tried to temper her excitement as she approached.

"Did you get your days mixed up or something?" Raq asked with a smile. "This ain't Monday, Wednesday, or Friday."

"Really?" Bathsheba gave the speed bag a final punch and put her hands on her hips, allowing her weary arms a brief rest. "I must have lost track of time." She stretched her arms to alleviate the lactic acid buildup in her shoulders, biceps, and triceps. "Your 'rows look good."

"Thanks." Raq ran her hand over her freshly braided hair. The cornrows were so tight she looked like she could barely blink. "I wanted to look good for my fight tomorrow night."

"You're fighting again? I thought you were injured."

"Not anymore." Raq flexed the fingers of her left hand to show they still worked. "Are you coming to watch me fight? Me and King's girl, Pepper, are going to be getting it on."

Pepper. That was a new name for Bathsheba to add to her growing list. She filed it away in her memory bank until she could get to her computer and store it permanently.

"I'd like to come, but I don't have a ticket."

"You know where to get one, don't you? Just go to Miss Marie's and ask for the Blue Plate Special."

Like their professional counterparts, Ice's fights were limited to ticketholders only. Similar to a rave, attendees weren't allowed entrance unless they could produce a piece of paper bearing the appropriate coded picture. The "tickets" were sold at the soul food restaurant Ice owned and had named for his mother, but unlike collard greens, fried chicken, and ox tails, they were definitely not on the menu.

"Are you gonna come?" Raq asked with a puppyish enthusiasm that made Bathsheba want to run a hand over her tight-ass braids like she used to do to her little sister before Mary pronounced herself too grown for such things.

"That depends." Bathsheba tried to play it cool despite her racing heart. "If I do, will you take me for that drink you promised me yesterday?"

"Sure," Raq said with a grin. "We can hit Club Peaches afterward, and you can help me celebrate my victory."

"Yo, Raq!" Zeke called out in the anachronistically deep voice that didn't match his slight frame. "Time is money. Get your ass in gear."

"I'd better go before he threatens to sic the old man on me," Raq said, looking uncharacteristically cowed. "I'll see you tomorrow night, right?"

Her eyes bore into Bathsheba's, seeking her approval. Bathsheba's handler had said there would come a time when the assignment would seem like too much. When she could no longer distinguish who she was from who she was pretending to be. She had said she could handle it. Now she had to prove it.

"I wouldn't miss it for the world."

CHAPTER FOUR

Raq could hear the buzz of the gathered crowd begin to grow louder as she went through her final preparations in the makeshift dressing room. The unheated warehouse was drafty and cold, but she had managed to work up a sweat nevertheless.

Even though she wasn't the headliner, she knew practically everyone in the house had come to see her. They wanted to know if she still had It. The indefinable something that separated her from everyone else. The thing that made her special when she stepped into the ring and made people keep their distance when she walked the streets.

"What are you going to do out there?" Zeke asked as she shadowboxed in a corner.

Exhaling through her nose, she snapped off two quick jabs followed by a roundhouse. "Stun her with the left and drop her with the right."

"That isn't what we agreed to."

Ice's cold, calculating voice made Raq shiver as if someone had just walked over her grave. Zeke stretched himself up to his full height to show he wasn't intimidated by Ice or the half-ton of muscle surrounding him. Ice and Zeke had never gotten along, and the tension between them had only gotten worse over the years. Raq knew she was the source of their conflict, but she didn't know how to resolve the problem in a way that would please both sides. Both said they wanted what was best for her, but she doubted anyone knew what that was, including her.

Ice tugged at the French cuffs peeking out of the sleeves of his tailored suit. "When we talked, I thought we agreed tonight's bout would last three rounds."

"It will," Raq assured him.

"Even if you tied one hand behind your back, this fight shouldn't go past the first round," Zeke said.

Ice slowly swiveled his head toward Zeke like a bird of prey zeroing in on its next meal. "If I were talking to you, I would have addressed you by name. Unless you hear me call your name, stay out of my business, punk."

Raq flinched at Ice's casual use of the derogatory slang term for a gay man. Zeke visibly bristled at the insult.

"If you put a leash on your dogs for five minutes, I'll bet this punk could kick your ass, you shiny suit-wearing motherfucker."

Hercules took a menacing step toward Zeke, but Ice held him back by holding up a hand in front of his beefy chest. "Chill, man. I paid too much for these shoes for you to ruin them by getting this little bitch's blood on them."

"Whatever, man," Zeke said.

Ice's smile didn't reach his eyes. "I need you to step outside for a few minutes, Ezekiel, so Raq and I can discuss business."

Zeke stood firm. "I'm not going anywhere, Isaac."

Raquel flinched inwardly. No one called Ice Isaac except his mama. "It's okay, Z," she said, stepping between him and Ice. "I'll be fine."

Zeke looked at her hard. "Girl, are you sure?"

"You heard the lady," Ice said.

Zeke waved him off. "You sure?" he asked again. Raq nodded. "All right then. I'll be right outside that door if you need me."

But they both knew that once he set foot out the door, Ice's bodyguards wouldn't let him back in.

"Stay strong," Zeke whispered before he left the room.

"Do I need to remind you about the terms of the agreement we made two days ago?" Ice asked.

"No, I remember. You want me to string this fight along until the third round before I drop the hammer."

Ice arched an eyebrow. "What if I said the terms had changed? What if I said I needed you to lose?"

Raq's heart sank. She had never lost a fight in her life. Hadn't even come close. Now Ice wanted her to drop one on purpose? How would that look? How was she supposed to score a big money fight against a man if she lost to a woman who was new to the game? "You want me to take a dive?"

Ice smiled suddenly. "No, girl. I was just kidding."

But Raq heard the unspoken coda to his statement. *This time.*

He placed a brotherly arm around her shoulders. "Now go out there and show the people what you can do." He tapped her chest with his fist. "Just don't do it too fast."

"You got it," she said with a grateful smile.

She was grateful because she knew she had dodged a bullet. Every other time Ice had asked someone to throw a fight, he hadn't rescinded the request. Her time would probably come one day, but today was not that day. She wanted to look good for the people who had ponied up their hard-earned money to watch her fight. And she wanted to look good for Bathsheba. Assuming Bathsheba had kept her word and showed up tonight.

Raq didn't know what she was looking forward to more—getting back in the ring again or taking Bathsheba out on the town after it was over. Easy. Going out with Bathsheba sounded a whole lot better than pretending to struggle against someone she could beat in her sleep.

But pretending to struggle was better than pretending to lose.

After Ice left, she picked up a towel and prepared to walk to the ring. She didn't know why Ice had suggested she spend her advance on a robe when he knew perfectly well the only accessory she wore to the ring was a towel with a hole cut in the center so it could drape over her shoulders, back, and chest just like Mike Tyson back in the day.

Zeke stuck his head in the door. "You all right?"

"It's all good."

"Cool." He looked relieved. She saw a flash of metal as he shoved his right hand in his pocket. Instead of bringing a knife to a gunfight, he had brought brass knuckles. Talk about old school. "I'll see you out there."

Zeke turned to leave. Since he wasn't part of Ice's crew, he couldn't accompany her to the ring. One of the few people she could depend on to always be there for her would be relegated to a seat in the audience instead of one in her corner. But that was okay. Because in the ring, the only person she could depend on was herself.

She opened the door and walked out. The noise hit her first. The smell soon followed. The sound of the announcer hyping up the crowd as he introduced the principals. The smell of greed, avarice, and good old-fashioned bloodlust. Shouting bettors waved bills in the air as she and her opponent approached the ring from opposite directions.

Pepper Martinez was big and strong with a long reach. She had earned a reputation as a brawler during a stretch in the pen, but Raq had seen enough of her fights since she'd been on the outside to know exactly how to beat her. Pepper telegraphed her punches, especially her right cross. All Raq had to do was wait for the big windup, slide to her right, and fire off a barrage of her own. To please Ice, though, she needed to spend the first two rounds pretending she couldn't find a way past Pepper's pathetic defense before she walked right through it in the third.

Raq climbed into the ring and raised her arms over her head to salute the cheering crowd. Dancing on her toes, she turned in a slow circle as she tried to spot Bathsheba in the audience. Her breath caught when she saw Bathsheba sitting in the third row looking fine as hell. She was wearing all black: boots, jeans, and a button-down shirt. Her hair was down, spilling on her shoulders and down her back. She wasn't wearing makeup, but her lips were painted an inviting shade of plum. Raq wondered if the rest of her was just as juicy.

In a few hours, she thought as Bathsheba returned her smile, I may get a chance to find out.

The referee was unlicensed, like everyone involved in the evening's events, but he looked the part as he called Raq and Pepper to the center of the ring. His instructions were close enough to the real thing to pass muster, but Raq zoned him out as she sized up her opponent.

Pepper had been representing King's crew for about six months. She was undefeated and all her wins had come by knockout, but Raq thought that had more to do with the quality of Pepper's opponents than her power. She'd know for sure, though, the first time she got hit.

"Touch hands, go to your corners, and come out fighting," the referee said.

"You're going down," Pepper said as she pounded her fists against Raq's.

"Is that a prediction or an invitation?" Raq asked, blowing her a kiss.

Pepper snarled and backed away. People who fought angry were easy to beat because they made too many silly mistakes and left themselves open.

"Three rounds?" Raq said under her breath. "I could take her out in three seconds."

When the bell rang, she was tempted to rush across the ring and show Pepper what real power was, but seeing Ice in his ringside seat reminded her what she had been asked to do.

Pepper came at her with a flurry of punches, windmilling her arms like a teenage girl in the middle of a schoolyard brawl. Raq either ducked the punches or let them bounce harmlessly off her shoulders. Halfway through the round, Pepper was gassed and holding on to her just to stay upright. When Raq pushed her off, Pepper nearly tripped on her own feet and went down.

"Do you want to change your prediction?" Raq asked after the bell rang to end the round.

Pepper's chest was heaving and she was breathing through her mouth, both signs of fatigue. "Next round."

Raq nearly laughed out loud. Maybe Ice was right. Stringing the fight along would increase Pepper's misery— and her enjoyment when she finally put her out of it.

As she stood in her corner, she watched money change hands, Ice's men collecting from people who had bet on a first-round knockout and come out on the losing end.

"When did you turn into a dancer, Raq?" someone called out as he grudgingly paid what he owed.

"Can you blame me?" Raq winked at him. "Take a look at my dance partner."

Pepper pointed across the ring and spit on the canvas. "Shut your fucking mouth, *puta*, or I'll shut it for you."

Pepper's visible anger riled up the fans even more. Ice smiled as more bets were laid down. Raq should have known better than to question his business sense, because when it came to making money, there wasn't anybody better at getting that shit done.

When the bell rang for round two, Pepper rushed her again. Raq turned all Floyd Mayweather on her, bobbing and weaving, landing a jab or two to piss her off, then dancing out of reach to piss her off even more.

"Are you going to run all night, or are you going to fight me?" Pepper asked after she managed to get her in a clinch.

Raq threw Pepper's own words back at her. "Next round."

She was so eager to get the fight over with, she almost couldn't stay in her corner between rounds. Pepper looked like she actually thought she had a chance to win, but she had no idea what she was in for.

The bell rang, signaling the third and final round. Raq turned to Bathsheba to make sure she was watching. Like they had been all night, Bathsheba's eyes were on her. Watching her. Seeing flashes of what she could do. Now she was about to see her at her best.

Raq looked at Ice to make sure there hadn't been a last-minute change in plans. When he gave her the nod, she felt like a kid on Christmas morning. She bulled forward and met Pepper in the center of the ring.

"It's about time."

Pepper smiled as if she'd finally gotten what she had been waiting for, but when she drew back to throw a right cross, Raq was the one who felt like celebrating. She took a step to her right and threw a short punch that landed on the side of Pepper's jaw. Pepper's eyes glazed over and she went down like she'd been shot.

Raq raised her arms in victory as the referee counted to ten. He could have kept going to a thousand and Pepper still wouldn't have gotten up in time. She was still woozy when a couple of King's men picked her up and dragged her toward her dressing room. Raq suspected she'd be seeing stars for a while. She'd clocked Pepper a good one and her hand still throbbed from the blow.

"That's my girl," Ice said. His voice was quiet, but it somehow carried over the roar of the crowd.

Raq sought out Zeke next. "You could have gotten that done in round one," he said. He was sitting with his arms and legs crossed and one foot was twitching like he had a nervous tic. He was frowning, but she could see the smile in his eyes.

"Next time."

She sought out Bathsheba last. Most of the females she kicked it with asked her why she did what she did. Bathsheba's expression said she already knew. For the sense of accomplishment that came from proving you were better at something than someone else was.

Raq patted the air with hands that had already started to swell. "Wait there. I'll be right back."

Bathsheba nodded in response.

Raq headed for the dressing room, accepting congratulations from well-wishers in the crowd as she went. She washed up with water from the sink, changed clothes, and joined Bathsheba in the audience. "You came," she said, taking a seat in the chair Bathsheba had saved for her.

"I told you I would. Didn't you believe me?"

Raq had grown so accustomed to people breaking their word she didn't know how to react when someone actually kept it. "You look good."

"Thanks. So do you."

Raq was wearing Tims, jeans, and a red Henley. She would have preferred a hoodie or her Ravens jersey, but the dress code at Club Peaches banned both. "Do you want to get out of here, or do you want to stay and watch the other fights?"

"Now that she's seen the best, why worry about the rest?" Ice asked in his Denzel Washington voice. Raq hadn't seen him walk up on them or sensed the crowd part to give him room. "Nice fight, Raq. Who's your friend?"

Raq felt Bathsheba stiffen next to her. Ice had that effect on people. She provided introductions like she was the hostess of some weird-ass cocktail party.

"I'm pleased to meet you, Bathsheba. Any friend of Raq's is a friend of mine." Ice stood back and gave Bathsheba an appraising look. "I hear you've been working out at Pop's. You look like you're in great shape. Do you fight?"

Bathsheba shrugged. "I've mixed it up a time or two. Just not in the ring."

"Do you want to get in the ring?"

"I haven't thought too much about it."

"You should. If you decide this is what you want to do, let me hook you up. I recognize potential when I see it, and I like to see it rewarded."

When Ice reached into his pocket and pulled out a business card, Raq hoped Bathsheba would refuse it. She didn't want her to get caught up in this business. Her face was too pretty to get rearranged.

Bathsheba turned the card over in her hands indecisively. "What would I have to do?"

"Whatever he tells you to do," Raq almost said.

"Raq can tell you how everything works. If what she says interests you, give me a call and we can talk specifics."

He was still using his Denzel voice. Raq hoped he didn't think he could use it to get into Bathsheba's drawers because she had already called dibs on those.

"Have a good evening, ladies. If you'll excuse me, I have some business I need to attend to."

Bathsheba looked starstruck as she watched him leave. Raq couldn't compete with Ice's money or his power. Few could. Raq lowered her head. She felt like Ice had stolen her shine.

Then Bathsheba turned to her and said, "How about that drink?"

CHAPTER FIVE

The music was bumping and the dance floor was crowded. While she waited for Raq to make her way back from the bar with their drinks, Bathsheba watched dozens of people perform the synchronized movements of the latest line dance. She knew how to do the usual party favorites—the Bus Stop, the Cha-Cha Slide, the Cupid Shuffle, and the Wobble—but the new dances were beyond her. They were fun to watch but hell to learn.

She could feel Ice's card burning a hole in her pocket. She wanted to pull it out and put it to use right away, but she didn't want to appear too eager. If she were as indecisive as she was pretending to be, she needed to let some time pass before she acted on the offer she had been given.

She wondered what Ice had in mind for her. Did he want her to be Raq's contemporary, or her successor? Did he want them to fight alongside each other or against each other? Raq was probably wondering the same thing. She hadn't had much to say during the short walk from Pop's to the club. Bathsheba was still trying to earn her trust, and it was already being tested. She needed to figure out how she was going to play this unexpected card she had been dealt and she needed to figure it out fast.

She walked the edges of the dance floor, trying to find an empty booth.

"Don't I know you from somewhere?"

The question made Bathsheba stop in her tracks. The club was packed, filled with people she didn't recognize, but someone had apparently recognized her. She slowly turned to see who had spoken, hoping against hope she wasn't about to come face-to-face with someone from her past.

The speaker was a young woman who didn't look old enough to drink, despite the colorful cocktail in her hand. Her clothes were too tight and too short, and either her heels were too high or her drink was too strong because she was unsteady on her feet.

"I do know you, don't I?" she asked with a hopeful smile.

"No," Bathsheba said, loosing a sigh of relief, "I can honestly say we've never met before."

"Oh, my bad."

"But keep trying, though. I'm sure there's someone here tonight who can't wait to get to know you."

"Thanks."

As Bathsheba slid into an empty booth, she remembered when she was young and yearning. She had made sure not to move too fast, but she didn't think her young friend could say the same.

"Was Cinnamon bothering you?" Raq asked when she finally showed up with the drinks.

"No, she was just saying hello." Bathsheba took a sip of her drink. Just a tiny one, though. Alcohol dulled the senses and she needed to keep her wits about her. "Cinnamon. Is that really her name?"

"Yeah. She has sisters at home named Sugar and Spice. They're twins, but they aren't identical."

"You're kidding me, right?"

Raq broke into a smile. "Yeah, I am, but I had you going for a minute, didn't I?"

"That you did."

Raq spread her arms across the back of the booth. "Are you going to take Ice up on his offer?"

Bathsheba tried to read her, but Raq's poker face was too good. "I don't know. What do you think I should do?"

Raq shrugged and reached for her drink. "What works for some people doesn't work for others. You might like it. You might not. Everybody's different."

"It works for you, though, right? You seem to be doing okay."

"I can't complain."

"So tell me how it works. Do you have a say in who you fight?"

Raq shook her head. "The promoters book the fights and the fighters fight. Sometimes, I don't know who I'm going up against until I step into the ring."

"How do you know what to expect?"

"I don't. That's what keeps things interesting."

"How's the money?"

"The money's good, but you won't get rich doing this, if that's what you're asking."

"So even if I say yes, I won't be trading my apartment in the complex for a penthouse downtown any time soon."

"Not unless you know something I don't."

"I doubt that. You've been at this a lot longer than I have."

"Are you thinking about doing this full-time or do you have a steady gig and you're just looking for some excitement?"

Bathsheba trotted out her cover story. "I do some office work part-time. It's a temp job that pays the bills, but it doesn't excite me, you know what I'm saying?"

"Yeah, I know. I saw your face tonight when I was in the ring. I could tell you know how good it feels to prove yourself against someone one-on-one. But have you thought about what you'd say to your boss if you showed up at the office with a black eye and a busted lip? If he thinks your boyfriend is tuning you up, he might march you down to the police station and make you fill out a report."

"I doubt it. Once he found out I prefer to date women, he stopped asking me questions about my personal life. But you're right. If I show up with bruises, I'll have to tell him something. What excuse do you use?"

Raq shifted in her seat. "I don't keep office hours, so no one cares what I look like during the day. Besides, I haven't had a black eye since I was fifteen and that one didn't come in the ring."

"How did it happen?"

Raq cracked her swollen knuckles. "My old man ran out when I was two. My mother had a string of boyfriends after he left. Her last one used to use me as a punching bag because I wouldn't put out for him. That shit stopped right quick as soon as Pop taught me how to lay that motherfucker out. Ice heard what happened and set me up with my first fight. The rest, as they say, is history. What's your story? Are your people from around here?"

"I grew up on Bradford Street, but we didn't stay in one place long enough to call any of them home."

"I hear you. Sounds like we both had it hard coming up."

"No doubt, but a difficult past makes for a sweeter present."

"I couldn't have said it better myself." Raq slid closer. "The day we met, you said I had to earn my time with you. How am I doing so far?"

"Well enough that you don't have to ask."

"That good, huh? Would you like to dance or should we skip straight to the after-party?"

Raq leaned in for a kiss, but Bathsheba stopped her by putting a finger against her lips.

"Why don't we try the appetizer before we start in on dessert?" She pulled Raq out of the booth and onto the dance floor.

"You're only delaying the inevitable, you know."

"What's the matter?" Bathsheba moved her body to the music, rolling her hips to the rhythm of the thumping bass line. "Don't you think I'm worth the wait?"

Raq's eyes moved hungrily over her. "I know you are. That's why I don't want to wait."

Teasing her, Bathsheba stroked Raq's earlobe and sensually ground her hips against her. When she felt Raq start to respond, she moved away. "What did you say in the ring? Next round."

Raq grabbed her and pulled her to her as the music slowed. "I'm going to hold you to that," she said as her hands locked around Bathsheba's waist.

Bathsheba ran her hands up the rippled indentations in Raq's stomach and circled them around her neck. "I hope you do."

Raq leaned back and gave her an appraising look eerily similar to the one Ice had given her back at the warehouse after Raq's fight. Raq not only took her cues from him, she seemed to get her moves from him as well. He was obviously much more than her employer. He was her mentor and idol as well. Coming between them might be harder than Bathsheba had expected.

"Do you want me to come with you when you talk to Ice?" Raq asked.

"I haven't made up my mind yet about meeting with him. How do you know I'll decide to hear what he has to say?"

"You'd be crazy not to. Look around. No one else around here is hiring. And if I go with you, I can make sure he offers you a good deal. It won't be as good as mine, but I'll see to it he treats you right. Then I can take you under my wing. Look out for you. Show you the ropes. Make you my protégée. Isn't that what they call it?"

"You'd do that for me?" Bathsheba stroked the back of Raq's neck, feeling the corded muscles move beneath her palm.

"That and a whole lot more. If you let me."

Raq's voice deepened and her eyes went dark. She leaned in for a kiss like she had in the booth. Bathsheba backed away once more, but she knew she couldn't put Raq off forever. She had to do enough to keep her interested, but how long would it take before Raq started asking for more?

"You mean to tell me I haven't earned a kiss yet?" Raq asked.

"Ask me after we talk to Ice and we'll see."

CHAPTER SIX

Bathsheba's brand new to the game, but I know she could be something special. You don't want her making money for someone else, do you? We need to lock her down before King gets his hands on her."

The leather chair creaked as Raq sat back in her seat. She wasn't much of a public speaker, but she thought she'd done a pretty good job laying out her case for bringing Bathsheba into the fold.

"*We?*" Ice snapped his fingers, and one of his bodyguards rushed over to refill his highball glass with Scotch. "Are you trying to be the leader of this outfit?" he asked after he took a sip of his fresh drink. "Because I thought that job was already taken."

"I'm not trying to step on your toes, Ice. I told Bathsheba I'd look after her, and that's all I'm trying to do."

"Did you take a trip to DC and get married or something? Because you're acting like she's your personal property."

"Nothing like that," Bathsheba said, the first words she'd spoken since she and Raq had set foot in the apartment. Raq turned to look at her. Bathsheba looked awed but not overwhelmed. That was a good sign. If she couldn't stand up for herself, she wouldn't last long. "Yes, Raq and I have been out once, but one date or a hundred, no one owns me."

Raq nodded in agreement. Bathsheba was fine, all right, but she wasn't trying to wife her up. She was glad they saw eye to eye. She couldn't imagine putting a ring on anyone's finger. What did marriage get you? Nothing, as far as she could tell, except pussy-whipped.

"That's good to hear." Ice turned his attention back to Raq. "Since you don't have a vested interest in today's proceedings, I need you to step out for a minute so Bathsheba and I can talk in private. Hercules will show you to the elevator."

Raq didn't move right away because she didn't think Ice was serious. He always sought her opinion of new fighters, and she participated in the meetings when he sat down with them. Why was he flipping the script now?

"If you say so," she said slowly.

"I do." He jerked his head toward the door, and Hercules took a step forward to make sure she got the hint. "Don't worry," Ice said after she reluctantly rose from her seat. "Your girl will be safe with me."

"What's so different about this one?" Hercules asked as he escorted her to the elevator. "Is Ice planning on grooming her to replace you or does he want a piece of that for himself?"

Raq shrugged as she jammed her hands into the pocket of her hoodie. "Your guess is as good as mine."

Hercules held his big hand inside the elevator to keep the doors from closing. "Wait downstairs until we call you back up. Try not to get arrested for loitering, okay?" he asked with a wink.

Raq flipped him off, but the gesture was lighthearted. Despite some of the things she'd seen him do at Ice's command,

Herc was a good guy. Probably the only one on Ice's payroll she'd trust to have her back if worst came to worst. The rest she wouldn't trust as far as she could throw them. And as big as most of these guys were, that wasn't very far.

"Keep an eye on her, okay? I don't want Ice to give her a test drive for the wrong part of the business."

"If he does decide to do that, what do you expect me to do except watch? He's the boss, remember?"

Yeah, she remembered. All too well.

Hercules removed his hand and the door slid shut. Raq rode it all the way to the bottom. Where, it seemed, she would always belong.

❖

Bathsheba rubbed her hands on the legs of her black slacks to force herself to sit still. What she wanted was in reach, but she needed to play it cool. She tried to make her excitement seem like nervousness. "Why did you want to talk to me alone?" she asked, casting a wary eye at Ice's cadre of armed guards.

He lit a cigar from the humidor on the coffee table and blew out a plume of fragrant smoke before he deigned to answer her question. "I wanted to get you by yourself because I didn't want Raq to hear what I had to say."

"Like what?"

"Where we come from, new faces don't stay new for long. I'd heard a lot about you even before Raq made her little speech extolling your virtues."

"What have you heard?"

She watched the bodyguards out of the corner of her eye. Was it her imagination or had Hercules crept closer to where she was sitting? She would have felt more comfortable having her service weapon on her, but she was glad she hadn't brought a gun because it might have been discovered when she and Raq were searched at the door, and she didn't know if she'd be able to offer a suitable explanation for its presence. She might not feel like it at the moment, but she was safer having her gun stashed back at the apartment.

"You're smart and you're independent, two of the qualities I admire in a woman. Before you get the wrong idea, I'm not trying to hit on you. You're a beautiful woman, but I don't want to cause friction between my employees."

"I think you already have."

He flinched as if he wasn't accustomed to being challenged. Most bullies weren't. "I'm afraid I don't know what you mean," he said, but Bathsheba suspected very little got past him.

"Raq didn't look happy when you kicked her out of here."

"She'll get over it. When she starts to forget her position, I have to remind her that this isn't a monarchy, and she isn't next in line for the throne."

"So who am I supposed to be, the court jester?"

Ice smiled around his Cohiba. "That depends on how you perform in the ring. If you embarrass me, I doubt either of us will be laughing. You feel me?" The question was obviously rhetorical because he didn't give her a chance to respond. "Now let's get down to business. Our deal is simple. You fight who I tell you to fight when I tell you to fight. I'll break you in slowly at first, but if you prove to be a draw, I'll make sure you have a spot on each card. Raq was my headliner and will be again as soon as she regains her old form, but there's plenty of money on the table for everyone."

"What's the split?"

"Since I pay for promotion, security, and various expenses, it's only natural I would receive the lion's share of the earnings. You get twenty percent of the action on the losing bets laid down for your fights."

"What about the gate? Isn't that where the real money is?"

He looked at her as if no one had ever dared to ask him the question. "One hundred percent of those profits go to the promoter whose fighters win the most bouts on a given night. In a way, I'm taking a gamble as well. Fortunately for me, I usually come out on the winning end. So do the people who work for me." He stood and beckoned for her to follow. He led her to a home gym filled with state-of-the-art workout machines that made the equipment at Pop's look obsolete in comparison. "All this could be yours to use for training. I make the same offer to all my fighters."

"Have any of them taken you up on it?"

"The ones who are serious about what they do."

"Raq seems pretty serious to me, yet she trains at Pop's."

Ice scowled momentarily before he arranged his features into a placid mask. "Raq feels she owes Zeke and his father something because they helped her out of a jam when she was younger. I allow her to indulge her fantasy because she's proven time and again her true loyalty is to me." He propped his foot on an elliptical machine. "Are you ready to join my team?"

Bathsheba almost said yes right away, but she forced herself to be cautious. "Where's the ring?" she asked, pointing out the only thing that was missing.

"I don't need one because I have this." He walked over to an interactive fitness machine equipped with six striking pads that tracked the speed of the user's punches and a speaker system that simulated the sounds of a sparring partner being hit. The onboard computer contained almost four hours of individualized workouts. The machine could do just about everything except fight back. Why would Raq train on the broken-down equipment at Pop's when she could be using this?

"Is there a contract I'm supposed to sign?" Bathsheba gave one of the striking pads a tentative punch that might have prompted the computer's electronic voice to taunt her like a real opponent would if the machine had been switched on.

Ice shook his shaved head. "I never write anything down. Not even a phone number. Paper trails lead only one direction—straight to prison. I'm not trying to go down that road."

The scant paper trail he had left behind led to nothing but dead ends. He hadn't left much of an electronic one, either. Everything related to his legitimate businesses checked out, and there was nothing to tie him to the businesses that weren't aboveboard. Wiretaps hadn't worked. Neither had round-the-clock surveillance.

Bathsheba suspected Ice laundered his drug money through Miss Marie's. Restaurants were cash-intensive businesses, which made it hard to prove when dirty money was being mixed in with the clean funds taken in over the counter. Either Ice or his accountant was probably smart enough to keep the restaurant's deposits under the ten-thousand-dollar reporting threshold, which kept Ice off the IRS's and the Feds' respective radars.

Major Crimes had been trying to follow the money for years. Every time they thought they were getting close, they veered off track. Now that Bathsheba knew tickets for the underground fights were being sold at Miss Marie's, the department had enough probable cause for a subpoena of the restaurant's financial records, but her handler had told her during their last meeting they wouldn't file the paperwork right away because they didn't want to raise Ice's suspicions while they had someone on the inside. Doing so could jeopardize both Bathsheba's chance of success and her life.

Ice was like an eel—too slippery to be caught. At least that's how most people saw it. Bathsheba, on the other hand, had a much different perspective. And she had come too far to let anyone or anything screw this up now.

"Count me in."

CHAPTER SEVEN

"You're not going to train at Pop's?" Raq asked after her second trip to the buffet. The Peking Gourmet was all-you-could-eat, and she wanted to make sure she got the most out of her money. Her plate was loaded with more than most people could eat, but she was just getting started.

"Ice's equipment seems pretty sweet," Bathsheba said.

"It is, but it doesn't teach you how to react to getting hit or correct what you're doing wrong."

That was what sparring partners and the watchful eyes of a knowledgeable trainer were for. Ice's fancy toys offered neither.

"Even so, I could never afford any of that stuff on my own. I would be crazy not to take advantage of a chance to use it for free."

Raq shoveled a forkful of fried rice into her mouth. "I'd hardly call it free. One way or another, he'll find a way to make you pay."

"As long as I get paid. That's all I care about. I'd hate to think I was doing all this for nothing. How do we get our money, anyway? Does Ice count it out in the dressing room after the fight or what?"

"Ice doesn't handle the payouts. Dez does. His guys count the profits from each fight and Ice decides who gets what. Then we meet up at Miss Marie's a couple days later and get paid. Some of the guys eat so much Ice might as well not pay them anything because most of the money goes right back into the till. Not me. A dinner at Miss Marie's costs ten bucks and lasts a few hours. Here, I pay seven and I can eat enough to last a whole day."

"What do you do with the rest of your earnings? Are you saving them for a rainy day?"

"The banks around here don't want my money, and if I stash it at my place, it would only get stolen. I let Zeke hold it for me. He gives me what I need and hangs on to the rest."

"You trust him like that?"

"He and Pop are more like family to me than my real family ever was. I owe Ice for giving me a livelihood, but I owe Pop and Zeke for giving me back my life."

"You told me a little bit about it at the club after your fight last week, but what exactly did they do for you?"

Raq chewed on an egg roll as she tried to suppress the unpleasant memories Bathsheba's questions had dredged up. "It's not something I like to talk about. Get me drunk enough and maybe I'll tell you."

Bathsheba smiled, showing off her dimples. "What am I supposed to do until then?"

"I could think of a bunch of things, but let's start in the ring. I want to see what you can do before the fists start flying for real. When's your first fight?"

"Two weeks."

"Then you'd better eat up because we don't have much time."

Bathsheba started in on her food. They'd been here for almost half an hour. She still hadn't finished her first plate and Raq was ready for thirds. "Does Dez handle all the payouts or just the ones to the boxers?"

"What do you mean?" Raq eyed the dessert buffet. She could use something sweet to round out her meal.

"Come on, Raq. I have eyes. I know boxing isn't all that Ice is into. How do the other people who work for him get paid, the dealers and hookers?"

Raq felt like she was betraying a trust until she remembered they were now working for the same man. "They get paid the same way we do. Not the same time, but the same way."

Bathsheba nodded as if Raq had just confirmed something she had already suspected. "So all the money flows through Miss Marie's?"

Raq pushed her empty plate away from her. "If you keep asking so many questions about Ice and his business, people are going to start thinking you're five-oh."

Bathsheba laughed. "Do I look like a cop to you?"

"No, but I'm not the one you need to convince. You don't have to worry about me."

"Who should I be worried about?"

"The ones who want what you have. Those are the people you need to watch out for."

"I shouldn't have anything to worry about in that regard because I don't have anything anyone would want."

"That's where you're wrong. You have a job, a place of your own, and you seem to be doing okay for yourself. Now you have something everyone around here wants: a spot in Ice's crew."

"You make it sound so glamorous. I'll have to remember that when I'm filing papers at my real job."

"At that copy place downtown?"

"How did you know where I worked?" Bathsheba's eyebrows knitted. Raq was afraid she'd react this way when she found out what Ice had put her up to.

"Ice asked me to find out."

"Do you know where I live, too?" Raq didn't say anything, but Bathsheba could tell by her silence that the answer was yes. She balled up her napkin and tossed it in her plate even though there was plenty of food left. "Do you do everything Ice tells you to do?"

"Everyone does, not just me," Raq said defensively. "Soon, you will, too."

"I doubt that."

"We all say that in the beginning. Then it gets harder and harder to say no."

Bathsheba narrowed her eyes as if she were trying to see inside her. "So you're saying there's nothing you wouldn't do?"

"Money talks. Bullshit walks. Everyone has a price."

"Is there a line you refuse to cross or would you do anything for the right amount?"

Raq had lost her appetite all of a sudden. She wasn't used to having to defend her actions or explain her motivations. It took her a minute to come to terms with the idea. The idea that she wanted acceptance and understanding from someone she barely knew when she didn't care if she received it from most of the people who had been in her life for years.

"Let's just say the other things he has on the menu aren't anything I would ever buy or sell."

"But you're willing to act as lookout for and offer protection to the ones who are willing to do what you won't? Is that better somehow?"

Raq looked at her hard. "How do you know about that?"

Bathsheba reached across the table and touched Raq's hand. Her fingers, soft and light, glided over Raq's knuckles. "Like I said, I have eyes. I know what you do when you're not in the ring, so you can stop trying to shield that part of your life from me."

Raq's fingers twitched involuntarily. She wasn't used to being treated with such gentleness. Her body didn't know how to react. "I didn't want you to look down on me because of what I do."

"We all have to make a living, right? I'm not here to judge you because of how you make yours."

Bathsheba took her hand away. Raq, already missing her touch, almost reached for her so she could go back to doing what she had been doing making her feel as normal as everyone else here. Bathsheba crooked her finger toward her as if she were summoning her across a crowded room instead of an intimate table for two.

"Come here. I think you've earned that kiss."

"Here? Now?"

Bathsheba cocked her head quizzically. "What's the matter? Aren't you out?"

"Yes, but what you said the first time we met has given me something to think about." Raq folded her arms on the table, enjoying going back-and-forth with someone who was just as skilled at running game as she was. "If I have to earn my kiss, you have to earn yours, too."

Bathsheba smiled and reached for her hand again. "What do I have to do?"

"Easy," Raq said, loving the idea of having something new to look forward to instead of the same-old, same-old day after day. "All you have to do is win your first fight. Now let's hit the gym so we can make sure that happens sooner rather than later. I don't want you to keep me waiting forever."

CHAPTER EIGHT

Bathsheba booted up her computer and started a Skype session. A few seconds after the program opened, the face of Bill Carswell, her handler, appeared on the screen. Everyone in the department called him Columbo because he always looked a little bit rumpled just like the private detective Peter Falk once played on TV, but today he looked positively haggard.

Carswell started to speak, but Bathsheba held up her hand, silently pleading for time to adjust the fit of the headset plugged into her computer's speaker jack. The apartment's walls were so thin she could hear every word of her neighbors' conversations. Unless she wanted to find herself in Ice Taylor's gun sights, she couldn't afford to return the favor.

"Is something wrong, Morris?" Carswell asked, running a hand through his already tousled hair.

"I'm meeting Raquel Overstreet at Pop's Gym in a few minutes for my first boxing lesson," Bathsheba said into the headset's microphone, "so I'm in a bit of a rush."

"What's going on? Tell it to me straight."

"I'm being followed, which means we have to stop using Copies Made E-Z as a meeting place. If someone sees you there and connects you to me, we're done."

"Who's got eyes on you?"

"Overstreet said Taylor asked her to check out my cover story."

"We knew that would happen at some point."

"Yes, but I thought I'd see them coming. Even though I knew what to look for, Overstreet managed to shadow me without my knowledge."

The admission made Bathsheba feel vulnerable. When she was on patrol, she had a partner to watch her back. Here, she was completely on her own.

"Let's not push the panic button yet," Carswell said. "As long as you stay a step ahead of your pursuers, you'll be fine." He rubbed his stubbled chin as if the action helped him think. "Do you still have the disposable cell phone I gave you?"

Bathsheba's eyes drifted to the ceiling as if she could see through it to what was hidden above the tile. "Yes."

"Then start using the burner to check in once a week and keep me up to date. If you feel like you're in over your head—"

"I won't."

"Fine. Let me put this another way. If you feel like they're on to you, let me know ASAP so I can pull you out of there."

Bathsheba's sense of duty overrode her concern for her own safety. "Thank you for that, sir, but I've got a job to do and I'm not going to stop until it's done. There's no way I'm going to let months of prep work go to waste."

"Your dedication's admirable, Morris, but don't be stupid." Carswell pointed at the screen like a lecturing father. "Ice Taylor's a dangerous character, and the people who work for him are no angels. If you sense trouble, get the hell out of there as fast as you can and don't look back. That's an order."

"Yes, sir. Same time next week?"

"I'll be waiting for your call."

She logged off the computer and shut it down. Before she could put it away, someone knocked on her door.

"Just a second."

She hurriedly climbed on the coffee table, lifted the ceiling tile, and hid the laptop. She let the tile fall and made sure it had settled smoothly into place before she climbed down and crossed the room to unlock the door. Without waiting to be invited in, Raq stepped into the apartment and looked around the living room.

"What's up?" Bathsheba asked, reaching for her duffel bag.

"I thought you had company."

"Why did you think that?"

"I heard you talking to someone."

Bathsheba forced her twitching hands to still as Raq looked at her distrustfully. "You probably heard me talking back to the TV," she said with a shrug. "I really get into my soaps."

Raq's tense features immediately relaxed into a smile. "I haven't watched the stories since *All My Children* went off the air. Erica Kane was my girl. Which show do you like?"

"*The Young and the Restless*," Bathsheba said quickly. She hadn't seen a single episode of the long-running show, but her roommate at the academy had been so hooked, it was all she could talk about. While Bathsheba had tried to study crime prevention techniques for the inner city, Ashley had gone on and on about the happenings in fictional Genoa City, Wisconsin. Bathsheba didn't know if the characters Ashley had told her about were still on the show, but she took a chance to make herself sound more convincing. "I can't believe some of the scrapes Victor and Nikki get into."

Raq nodded knowingly. "I had to stop watching them because they reminded me of too many people I know. They make each other miserable when they're together, but they can't stand to be apart. You ready to go? I figured we'd get in some ring work at Pop's today and head to Ice's place tomorrow for a workout."

The abrupt change in subject let a relieved Bathsheba know Raq believed her story. This time. As they began to walk to the gym, Bathsheba felt like she'd dodged another bullet. How many more could she avoid before she encountered one that had her name on it?

❖

Raq leaned on the ring apron as she listened to Zeke call out instructions.

"Keep your hands up. Tuck in your chin. Stay on your toes. That's the way."

Bathsheba pushed her padded headgear out of her eyes as she stalked her sparring partner, a southpaw with fast hands but not a lot of power. He could pile up points, but he couldn't knock anyone out, which made him the perfect person for her to test herself against. She could feel what it was like to get hit, but she wouldn't be in any danger of getting her bell rung.

Raq had expected Bathsheba to look lost when she climbed into the ring for the first time, but she looked good in there. Like she knew what to do even though she had to be reminded to do it.

"Don't let him run circles around you," Raq said. "Cut him off and force him into a corner."

Zeke tossed a sweat-dampened towel in her direction. "Who's teaching this class, me or you?"

"Sorry, Z. Do your thing."

Bathsheba tapped her gloved hands against her headgear and closed in on her grinning opponent. Before she could erase the distance between them, the timekeeper banged a tiny metal hammer against the ringside bell.

"Stop!" Zeke, acting as referee as well as instructor, stepped between the combatants to make sure one didn't sucker punch the other. "All right, you two. Get some water and hit the showers. That's enough for one day."

Bathsheba and her sparring partner touched gloves and headed to their respective corners. "How did I do?" she asked after she spit out her mouthpiece.

Raq squeezed water into Bathsheba's open mouth. "Are you sure you haven't been in the ring before?"

"I was about to ask the same thing." Zeke loosened Bathsheba's gloves and removed them with a jerk. "You're rusty, but you've got mad skills."

Bathsheba unfastened her headgear and pulled it off. Then she opened her mouth for more water and drank greedily. "I've been a fight fan for a long time, but I'm not a fighter myself," she said, wiping excess water off her chin.

Zeke tied the gloves together and draped them over his shoulder. "You must be a natural then because you look like you've been doing this all your life. When's your first fight?"

"Friday after next. I don't know where yet, though, or against whom."

"Wherever it is, I'll be there. I'm not a betting man, but if I were, I wouldn't bet against you. Same time tomorrow?"

"No," Raq said quickly. "She wants to try out some of Ice's fancy toys, so we're going to head to his place tomorrow."

"I see." Zeke looked like someone had just told him Club Peaches had gone under just like most of the other businesses in the neighborhood.

"Are you going to tell Pop?" Raq asked as Zeke climbed out of the ring.

He paused on the bottom step and looked back at her. "What do you think?" he asked, his upper lip curled into an angry snarl. Zeke didn't get mad often. When he did, it wasn't a pretty sight.

"I think what he doesn't know won't hurt him."

"That's one thing we agree on." Zeke's shoulders slumped as if he bore the weight of the world on them. He was much too skinny to be carrying around such a heavy load. "See you when I see you."

Raq's relief that he wouldn't rat her out was mixed with the familiar disappointment she felt each time she had to keep one part of her life separate from the other.

"Antoine," Zeke said, capturing the attention of a young flyweight with a small frame but big dreams. "Tie your shoes before you trip and break your neck."

Whenever Zeke raised his voice, the only correct response was immediate compliance. Instead of talking back, the kid stopped jumping rope, dropped to one knee, and tied his tennis shoes, which were worn fashionably loose like the dealers ruling the streets of the neighborhood.

Bathsheba rested her arms on the ring ropes. Even though she had sparred for a full three rounds, she wasn't even breathing hard. She had the stamina to be a good fighter, but her chin was still untested. Raq needed to see her take a good, solid punch right on the button before she could start considering her as competition. If then. Despite Bathsheba's obvious talent, Raq still thought she could take her in a fight because she had something Bathsheba didn't: nothing to lose. Bathsheba was educated with a job she could be proud of. Her book smarts could lead her out of the 'hood. The only way Raq could escape was to fight her way out.

"I don't want to cause a rift between you and Zeke," Bathsheba said. "I can work out at Ice's by myself. I don't need you to come with me."

"I know you don't need me to, but I was hoping you wanted me to."

Raq wasn't big on socializing, but she liked hanging out with Bathsheba. And she didn't want her going to Ice's place alone. Ice would put his guys in check if any of them got out of line, but Raq wanted to do it herself to make sure they got the point.

"Of course I want you to come with me, but if it's going to be a problem for you and Zeke—"

Raq held up her hands. She was used to instilling fear, not easing it. "Stop worrying. Zeke and I are always going to be cool. No one could ever mess that up, all right?"

"All right." Bathsheba showed off those dimples of hers. Every time she saw them, Raq felt them draw her in a little bit closer. Soon, there might be no turning back. "What do we do next?"

Raq didn't know about Bathsheba, but she knew what she wanted to do. She wanted to claim the kiss she'd been waiting for, but her phone rang before she could finally take what was hers.

She pulled the phone out of the front pocket of her loose-fitting jeans. She didn't recognize the number on the display, but that was nothing new. Ice bought a new set of burners every month and had everyone ditch their old ones, so she didn't bother memorizing anyone's digits once she programmed them into speed dial. The code she had attached to the number let her know the caller was Half Pint.

"Wassup, man?"

"Little Tony caught a case of the blue flu. I need you to come to the spot and watch my back."

Half Pint's voice was reedy and panicked. Raq could hear the fear he was trying to hide. He and Tony were tight. Seeing his partner getting tossed into the back of a cop car must have been like seeing himself get popped.

"Did you tell Ice what happened?"

"Yeah. He's the one who told me to call you. He's sending a lawyer to the police department to see if he can spring LT, but the cops caught Tony with two bags in his pocket, so I think he's going to be stuck in the can for a while. Forget about him, though. I need to take care of me and mine. You coming down here to handle your business or what?"

"Where are Winky and One-Eyed Mike?"

"Don't know, don't care. If you were in my place, would you want a couple of dudes who are blind in one eye and can't see out the other looking out for you? Because I sure as hell don't. Besides, Ice asked me to call you and that's what I'm doing. Do you want me to call him back and tell him you're too busy getting your nails done to help his top earner out of a jam?"

Raq had known Half Pint long enough to know his threat to bring Ice into play wasn't an idle one. Sometimes the little runt acted like he was driving the ship when he was nothing but a passenger just like she was.

"Calm down, dude. I'm on my way."

"That's more like it."

"Do you have to go to work?" Bathsheba asked after Raq ended the call.

"Yeah. I don't know how long I'm going to be, so I won't make any promises about trying to hook up with you later. I'll see you at Ice's tomorrow, okay? Same time as today."

"Okay."

Raq turned to leave. Because she had planned to watch instead of work out, she was still wearing her street clothes, which made it easy to make a fast transition from doing what she loved to what she hated.

"Hey," Bathsheba said.

Preoccupied with her own thoughts, Raq turned back to see what Bathsheba wanted.

"Be careful out there."

Bathsheba grabbed a handful of Raq's oversized sweatshirt and held her fast. Raq's first instinct was to try to free herself because she hated being anyone's prisoner, real or imagined. But when Bathsheba leaned forward and pressed her lips against hers, she didn't want to be anywhere else. She moved forward, melting into the kiss. Drowning in it.

She felt herself going under. She wanted to stay there, but she forced herself to come up for air.

"I gotta go," she said hoarsely.

"Are you all right?"

Bathsheba's eyes were filled were concern. She reached out with one bandaged hand, but Raq pulled away from the attempted caress. Despite how much she wanted to stay with Bathsheba—to allow herself to be touched by her—she had made a previous commitment she couldn't afford to break. Whenever the streets called, she had to answer.

"Yeah, it's all good, but I gotta go."

Bathsheba frowned and fisted her hands on her hips in disapproval. Raq slowly backed away to make sure Bathsheba didn't intend to follow her, then she turned and rushed out. On the sidewalk, she flipped the hood of her sweatshirt over her head and affixed the scowl she used to keep rivals at bay. But the expression that once seemed so natural now felt like a mask. A mask that kept turning into a smile every time she allowed herself to think about Bathsheba Morris.

Bathsheba's kiss had affected her in ways both expected and not. In addition to making her want a slow-motion replay, the kiss was making her do something she hadn't done in a very long time: dream of a life far different from the one she knew. The only one she had ever known.

The streets are calling, she thought as she ran to stand lookout over Half Pint until he sold the rest of the inventory he had been allotted for the day, but they don't have to be my home.

With someone like Bathsheba by her side, she could go places. Be somebody.

"Who do you think you are, Jesse Jackson or some shit?" she asked, laughing at herself before someone could do it for her. "You were born on these streets, you live on these streets, and you're going to die on these streets. If you let a pretty face soften you up, your time could come a lot sooner than you want it to."

When her mask fell into place this time, it felt like she did every morning when she woke up in the Middle East: like it belonged there.

CHAPTER NINE

Bathsheba checked her watch as she worked out on an exercise bike programmed to mimic the terrain displayed on an attached projection screen. The majestic mountain trail was jaw dropping in its beauty and probably could have captured her attention for hours if she didn't have other things on her mind.

Raq was late. They had agreed to meet at Ice's apartment at noon, but it was well past one and Raq still hadn't showed. Bathsheba told herself not to be worried—Raq had been running the streets for years with no issues—but she was a woman of her word, and Bathsheba didn't think she would break it without unwanted help.

Bathsheba turned to Bigfoot, who was turning the pedals of his own exercise bike at almost glacial speed.

"Have you heard from Raq?"

"Not since the last time you asked me that question," Bigfoot said breathlessly, his bulk shifting from side to side as his legs slowly churned.

His sweat-soaked T-shirt clung to his massive chest and shoulders. He watched the scenery on the screen with the gimlet-eyed wonder of a kid sprawled in front of his favorite

Saturday morning cartoon. His obvious fascination with the bike and its high-tech accessories made it clear he didn't use the apparatus often, if at all, which let Bathsheba know his presence at her side was deliberate instead of coincidental. Just like he'd done with Raq, Ice had asked Bigfoot to keep an eye on her. Smart move since Bigfoot's surveillance kept her from performing a great deal of her own. Instead of using her camera phone to document the penthouse's layout, she was being forced to commit it to memory until she could return to her apartment and sketch it out for her records.

Memories and impressions would do for some parts of her investigation. For the rest, however, she would need tangible evidence. Photographs. A recording. Something—anything—she could use to make sure Ice Taylor finally paid for his life of crime. What she had so far was a good start, but it was mostly circumstantial. She didn't have nearly enough to make a solid case. She needed more. But with all these eyes on her, how was she supposed to get it?

What she wouldn't give to be able to film her visit today. If her visits became more frequent, perhaps she could figure out a way to set up a hidden camera in her duffel bag. It was a risky move, considering Ice's bodyguards searched her and her belongings the instant she set foot in the door, but their searches weren't as thorough as some she had endured. If she found a camera that looked like something innocuous instead of what it really was, perhaps she could get away with sneaking it inside.

She looked away from Bigfoot and turned back to the projection screen attached to her bike, seeking but unable to find solace in the images displayed there. "Raq didn't get into any trouble, did she? I heard on the news this morning there was a shooting in the Middle East late last night. An unidentified man's body was found dumped in an alley. The newscaster said he was shot execution style. Since Raq doesn't carry, she's defenseless when she's on the street."

"She's at a disadvantage, but I wouldn't call her defenseless. In a fair fight, she can knock a motherfucker out like nobody's business."

"When was the last time you heard of anyone on that corner fighting fair? Guns are the great equalizer."

"True that. True that." Bigfoot nodded his head like a bobblehead doll as he continued to huff and puff. Then he shrugged his thick shoulders helplessly. "Raq should carry a piece since everyone around her is strapped up, but she made a choice not to. That isn't a move I would make. I'm not into that old school shit. I don't even go to the crapper without my nine. But she's grown. She can do what she wants." He paused to catch his breath. "As for the shooting, none of our people were involved. If they had been, someone would have called Ice and he would have sent Dez to take care of it. Since both of them are playing video games in the front room, I don't think there's a problem. Now, if you're done asking me fifty million questions, I'm going to get something to eat. All this exercise is making me hungry." He climbed off the bike and hitched up his baggy sweatpants. "You want something?" he asked, toweling off his sweaty face and neck.

"No, I'm good."

"Ice's refrigerator looks like Noah's ark. He's got two of everything. Are you sure you don't want me to hook you up?"

"Maybe when I'm done working out. I've got a rhythm going and I don't want to stop."

"Damn. My college coaches would have loved you. During practice, they made me keep going until I puked or passed out."

Bigfoot ran the towel under his armpits, pressed it to his nose, then draped it over his shoulder. Bathsheba was a bit grossed out by the display, but chose to take his comfort in her presence as a positive sign. Once she earned his trust, she could start taking advantage of it.

"Do you miss your days on the playing field?" she asked. She thought she'd heard a hint of nostalgia in his voice when he talked about the past.

"When I fucked up my knee, my homies were acting all sad because I wouldn't be coming into pro money and they'd be missing out on a free ride, but I was happy it happened, you know what I'm saying?"

"Why?"

"I was tired of getting yelled at all the time and being told what to do. Tearing my ACL was the best thing that ever happened to me."

Bathsheba waited in vain for him to realize the irony of what he had just said. How was bending to Ice's will any different from doing his coaches' bidding? And why did he find one more palatable than the other?

Her heart ached at the thought of his wasted potential. Not just his. So many people in Ice's orbit could have made something of themselves if Ice hadn't insinuated himself into their lives. Raq and Bigfoot had athletic ability. Dez had an affinity for numbers. All could have had successful careers in a legitimate field, yet they had chosen to embark on paths that would most likely end with them dead or in jail. All because Ice Taylor had convinced them to sacrifice their dreams for his vision. His considerable charm was even deadlier than the product he sold.

"Keep pedaling. I'll be back after I rustle up some grub," Bigfoot said.

He hitched up his pants again and lumbered out of the room, limping slightly on his damaged left knee. He had lasted a lot longer on the exercise bike than Bathsheba thought he would, but his surprising stamina had cost her valuable time. Time she could have put to much better use.

She cocked her head to see if Ice and Dez were engaged in meaningful conversation she needed to track. She heard the sounds of digitally rendered warfare and testosterone-fueled competition, but nothing about business. Ice and Dez were acting like a couple of buddies sharing a few laughs, not the leaders of a vast criminal organization. She wondered if they were putting on an act for her benefit or if they conducted business meetings somewhere other than here. Someplace like Miss Marie's.

Bathsheba needed to explore the restaurant's offices and back rooms. If the money for the payouts was housed there, perhaps other, more incriminating evidence resided there as well. Namely the location of the building Ice used to store his drugs and the names and contact numbers of his suppliers. If she could, she wanted to put them out of business as well. Though it wouldn't completely eradicate the drug problem, it would go a long way toward stamping it out.

She and Raq would be at Miss Marie's this weekend, looking to get paid for their respective fights on Friday night. Bathsheba didn't expect to earn much, but any intel she uncovered while she was onsite might prove invaluable. She checked her watch again, even though she knew only a few minutes had passed since the last time she'd performed the same action.

"Where are you, Raq?" she said under her breath.

In a way, she should have been glad Raq was MIA. She could perform a still limited but marginally more thorough reconnaissance of Ice's apartment with one less person around to keep tabs on her, but she was too distracted to take advantage of the opportunity she'd been afforded.

She was loathe to admit it, but she needed Raq more than she had ever needed anyone in her life.

She had managed to find her way inside Ice's crew, but her connection to the members of Ice's inner circle was tenuous at best. She needed Raq to get her closer. Raq getting hauled off to jail or taken out by someone working for a rival dealer were complications she couldn't afford. Raq was integral to the successful completion of her assignment. Bathsheba couldn't achieve one without the help of the other. At the moment, though, she was more concerned about Raq than the case.

She closed her eyes and tried to visualize each room in Ice's apartment so she could force her mind to focus on what was important. Ice was her target. Raq was nothing more than the means to an end. Except she was starting to feel like something more.

As she moved from the exercise bike to the weight bench, Bathsheba reflected on the kiss she had impulsively instigated the day before. The kiss had been meant to pique Raq's interest. In the process, it had sparked her own.

She couldn't remember the last time she was in a relationship that had lasted longer than a few months. Ever since she had graduated from the police academy, she had kept to herself except for a handful of one-night stands and brief flings that ended almost before they began.

Women were attracted by her uniform, but the danger inherent to her profession drove them away. She couldn't blame them for leaving. And as much as she might have wanted some of them to stay, she couldn't ask someone to risk her heart on her knowing she might not make it home after the end of her shift.

She and Raq were on opposite sides of the law, but they had one thing in common. As today proved, there was no guarantee Raq would make it home safely at the end of the night either. Had she, like Bathsheba, made a decision to keep love at bay or was she willing to open herself up in ways Bathsheba wasn't? The answer, Bathsheba knew, could affect not only the outcome of the case, but the direction of her life as well. She didn't know how to feel about either prospect. And she didn't know how she was supposed to feel about Raq.

Raq was rough around the edges, but tender at the center. She was like a decadent dessert: bad for you in so many ways, but oh-so-sweet on your tongue. Bathsheba was drawn to her. Attracted to her. Two things she hadn't expected to happen. Not this soon.

She had been told to expect to grow close to the people she was pretending to befriend. Most undercover officers did at some point. Some even started families with people they became acquainted with while they were living under assumed identities. But she hadn't expected it to feel like this. She hadn't expected it to feel so real.

"It's all an act," she reminded herself as she hoisted a metal bar containing fifty pounds of weight on each end.

But spending time with Raq felt like anything but an act. Certainly, their first encounter at Pop's Gym had felt artificial. So had the beginning of their date at Club Peaches. But once they'd starting sharing each other's stories, the dynamic had changed. Bathsheba hadn't felt like a police officer working a potential informant. She had felt like a woman being treated to a night out by someone who wanted to take the time to get to know her better instead of rushing into something fleeting. The feeling was intoxicating, but Bathsheba needed to keep her head on straight to keep it from getting chopped off.

"Stick to the script," she said under her breath. "Stick to the script."

A burst of raucous laughter from the living room made her assume the video game had reached or was nearing its conclusion.

"Time to look busy."

She lowered the weight to her chest and exhaled forcefully as she extended her arms until her elbows locked. Then she repeated the process once, twice, three times. The weight grew heavier and her arms more rubbery with each repetition.

"Don't you know you're not supposed to do bench presses without a spotter?"

Bathsheba was so surprised to hear Raq's voice—to see her standing safe and sound in the open doorway—she nearly dropped the hundred pounds of weight in her hands.

"Whoa. Take it easy. I got you." Raq dropped her duffel bag on the floor and ran across the room. "There we go," she said as she helped Bathsheba lower the bar onto the metal catchers on each side of the weight bench. "How long have you been at it?"

"Long enough." Bathsheba sat up and reached for the water bottle she had stowed under the bench. "Where have you been?" she asked after she took a long swallow.

Raq backed up a step as if she had been caught off guard. "I had something I needed to take care of."

"Something like what?"

No longer giving ground, Raq dug in her heels and looked at her hard. "What's with the third degree?"

"I was worried about you," Bathsheba almost said, but she sensed that wasn't the right way to play the game. "My first fight is coming up in a few days. That might not mean much to you since you've been through this more times than I have, but I don't want to fuck things up my first time out. If you don't want to take this seriously, that's fine. I can ask someone else to help me."

"Who, Bigfoot?" Raq snorted laughter. "You put such a whipping on his ass today, he's in the kitchen passed out in a plate of smoked turkey necks. If you want a real workout partner, I'm your girl."

"Then act like it."

Bathsheba tried to walk away, but Raq grabbed her arm before she could get too far.

"Hold on."

"Don't," Bathsheba said, pulling free.

"Come on. Don't be like that." Raq's tone was wheedling, but Bathsheba turned her back on her to show she wasn't swayed by the attempt to beg her forgiveness. "What do you want me to do, huh?" Raq asked with an exasperated sigh. "What do I have to say to make things right between us?"

Bathsheba turned to face her. "You can start by telling me why you're almost two hours late for our appointment. And don't try to give me some bullshit excuse like you overslept because that isn't going to cut it."

Raq stood firm again. "Do you really want to know where I was?" she asked defiantly.

"If I didn't want to know, I wouldn't have asked you, would I?"

"Fine. I'll tell you."

Raq leaned toward her like a drill instructor trying to intimidate a new recruit. Bathsheba could understand why most of Raq's opponents seemed beaten even before the bell rang to start the fight.

"A john wasn't satisfied with the service he received from one of the girls and he demanded a refund. He laid into her when she wouldn't give him his money back. I had to tune him up to reinforce the fact that all sales are final. The way Honey looked after he was finished with her, he's lucky I didn't do more than give him a busted nose and two black eyes. While you were here riding tricycles and lifting weights, I was out in the streets putting in real work. That's where I was. Are you happy now?"

Raq's anger was mixed with a healthy dose of desperation Bathsheba found all too familiar. Though she empathized with Raq's distress, she couldn't let it distract her from trying to gather information. "What about last night's shooting? Were you involved? Did you see it?"

"No, I wasn't involved. And, yeah, I saw it." Backing off, Raq rubbed a hand across the back of her neck as if to ease growing tension. "Watching someone's brains get splattered on the sidewalk isn't the kind of thing you forget easily. That's why I don't carry a piece, man. It's too easy to do something you can't take back. You can apologize for busting someone's nose, but there's nothing you can say to make up for taking someone's life. Once you pull the trigger, that's it."

"Did you know the man who was killed?" Bathsheba asked gently. "Was he one of ours?"

Raq shook her head forlornly. "He wasn't a dealer. He was a customer. Or pretending to be."

That got Bathsheba's attention. Was someone from the vice squad trying to horn in on her investigation, or were the dealers in the Middle East so paranoid they saw danger in every unfamiliar face? She wanted to solicit Carswell's opinion on the matter, but she wasn't scheduled to speak with him for several more days. Until then, she would have to follow her own instincts. Her gut told her to press the issue rather than let it drop. "What do you mean pretending?"

"I didn't know the guy. He was new to the corner, but Double D—the dealer he was trying to cop from—must have thought he was five-oh or something because he gave him two to the head without even thinking twice."

Double D. Bathsheba recognized it as the street name belonging to Dwayne Davidson, a member of King's crew. If he was slinging in the Middle East, he was outside King's territory. Bathsheba wondered if a turf war was in the offing. If so, she was positioned to get caught right in the middle of it.

"Everyone scattered after Double D started letting off shots," Raq continued. "I made sure my boys were okay, then I went home and tried to wash what I'd seen off me. I scrubbed until my skin felt raw, but I still don't feel clean." She ran her hands over her arms as if reliving the attempted baptism.

"Raq, I'm—"

Bathsheba reached for her, but Raq pulled away.

"I don't want you to see that side of my life," Raq said, her eyes shining with unshed tears. "I'm trying to protect you from the ugliness that's out there in the world. Why won't you let me?"

"Because I want to see you. All of you." Bathsheba took Raq's hands in hers and gently rubbed her bruised knuckles. She sought to comfort as well as interrogate. "How can I see you when you keep trying to hide part of yourself from me?"

Raq looked at her wordlessly for a moment, either sizing her up or trying to figure her out. If Bathsheba didn't convince Raq she was on the up-and-up, hers might be the next body found abandoned in an alley.

"I've never met anybody like you," Raq said at length. "What's your game?"

"I'm not trying to play games. I'm being straight up with you, Raq, and I hope you can be the same with me, all right?" Raq took her time before she finally nodded her assent. Bathsheba gave her hands a gentle squeeze and let them go. "Cool. Now let's get down to business. I've got a fight to win."

CHAPTER TEN

R aq didn't get nervous before her own fights, but she was petrified now. Bathsheba was scheduled to enter the ring in a few minutes, and Ice hadn't made it easy for her. Instead of matching her up against a pushover to build her confidence and guarantee an easy victory in her first fight, he and the other promoter had put her in with Sabrina Guthrie, one of the dirtiest fighters in the game. Sabrina didn't care about what she had to do to win a fight as long as the referee raised her arm after the decision was announced.

"When the referee tells you to protect yourself at all times, it ain't no joke," Raq said as Bathsheba jumped rope to work up a sweat. "Sabrina will do whatever it takes to win. Remember that movie where Clint Eastwood trains Hilary Swank to be a boxer? Sabrina puts the bitch who broke Hilary's neck to shame. We fight bare-knuckled because it ups the risk and brings in more bets. Even though it's technically against the rules, Sabrina used to wear padded MMA-style gloves in the ring. Ice and the rest of the promoters let her keep them because they were her trademark. The fighters were cool with it, too. Until she got caught loading up her gloves with ball bearings. She turned one girl's face into mush once by doing that. The officials are supposed to check for shit like that before each bout, but some of them are so shady they'll let anything slip by for a fee. If Sabrina comes to the ring with her hands wrapped, don't let her get them anywhere near your eyes because she's probably soaked the bandages in liniment so she can blur your vision long enough to knock you out."

"If she's so bad, why is she allowed in the ring?" Bathsheba said between puffs of air as she continued to skip rope.

"Because she puts butts in the seats. Crowds love having someone to root against, and she makes it easy for them to find someone to hate. They turn out just to see what she'll do next."

Bathsheba laughed as she twirled the rope one last time. "I feel like a gladiator about to enter the arena."

"They don't call boxing a blood sport for nothing."

JoJo, the other female member of Ice's stable on the card tonight, tossed her street clothes in her locker and slammed the dented metal door. "You're full of advice now, but you didn't have shit to say when I was new to the game. What's the matter? I didn't shake my ass right or something?"

Raq felt her temper flare. She hated when people tried to rewrite history to make themselves look good instead of telling it how it really was. "I tried to tell you things, but you didn't want to listen. You thought you knew everything."

A smirk slowly crept across JoJo's face. "You think you know it all, don't you? If you think I don't know some things you don't, you'd better think again. Or, better yet, why don't you ask him?"

JoJo jerked her chin toward the door, where Ice's distinctive profile was displayed on the pebbled glass. Before Raq could ask JoJo what she was trying to say, Ice tapped on the door and came inside without waiting for a response. Dez followed him in while their bodyguards stood outside the door.

"How are you lovely ladies doing this fine evening?" After Raq, Bathsheba, and JoJo murmured variations of the same positive response, Ice spread his arms and said, "I don't mean to interrupt your preparations, but we need to take care of something before you get down to business."

He nodded at Dez, who stepped forward with a plastic grocery bag in his hands. When he reached into the bag, Raq hoped he'd come out with something good. Instead, he pulled out three home pregnancy tests and started handing them out.

"What's this?" Raq asked, turning the box over in her hands.

"New rule," Ice said. "No female can go into the ring unless she passes one of these tests first. One of King's girls didn't let on she was in the family way until she ended up in the hospital after her last fight. I don't want to have history repeat itself. But that isn't something I need to worry about because I know none of my girls would keep something like that from me, would they?"

Raq and Bathsheba assured him he had nothing to worry about, but JoJo was strangely quiet.

"You got something you want to tell me, JoJo?" Ice asked.

Raq's stomach sank when Ice cocked his head. Whenever he did that, it meant something bad was about to happen.

Her eyes downcast, JoJo delicately placed the box containing the pregnancy test on the bench. "Can we talk about this in private?"

"There's nothing you need to say to me you can't say in front of my people. What's up?"

"Um." JoJo scratched her head as if she was trying to dig up the right answer to Ice's question. "I was going to tell you."

"When? When you started to show? What kind of business do you think I'm running here? Your fight's canceled and so are you." He snapped his fingers. Bigfoot and Winky stepped forward. "My associates will show you out."

"But I thought we were tight," JoJo said as Bigfoot and Winky took her by the arms and began to drag her out of the room.

"You thought wrong."

"You know the baby's yours, right?"

"Oh, snap," Raq said. She had no idea Ice and JoJo had been kicking it. She knew he used to get around, but she thought he had kept his dick on lockdown since he and the Black Dahlia had started knocking boots.

Ice turned on JoJo, his voice as cold as his name. "Like I said, you thought wrong."

JoJo's eyes pleaded with him to change his mind, but she was old news as soon as the door closed behind her.

"What are you two waiting for?" Dez asked. He pointed toward the toilet stalls at the back of the room. "Hop to it."

"Are you serious?" Raq asked. "You know how I roll. All the girls I've been with are shooting blanks. I don't need this."

She tried to hand the box back, but Dez wouldn't take it.

"Miracles happen. Now go piss on a stick and pray it doesn't turn blue."

Raq dutifully opened the home pregnancy test and headed to a toilet stall. Bathsheba took the stall next to hers. Raq watched Dez's alligator shoes pace back and forth outside the stall as she held the test stick under her and tried not to pee on her hand. "Is someone going to take JoJo's place tonight or are we going to forfeit the fight?"

"And lose out on a chance to make some money? Screw that. Ice and I were thinking. We're going to watch both your fights. Whoever has the more impressive showing will earn a chance to double her money tonight. How does that sound?"

Raq didn't like the idea of taking money out of Bathsheba's mouth, but she could use the extra bread.

"It sounds like you'd better get ready to pay me."

She opened the stall door and tossed Dez the negative test. Dez jumped back as if she'd thrown a bucket of urine at him.

"Congratulations," he said, carefully holding the test stick between two fingers. "You get paid tonight." He dropped the test stick into a plastic bag like he was a cop collecting evidence at a crime scene. Then he banged on the door to Bathsheba's stall. "How's it coming in there? You didn't drown, did you?"

Bathsheba flushed the toilet and unlocked the door. "Shy bladder."

Dez glanced at the test stick before he bagged it up. "Two for two. Now let's make this money."

"Bet," Raq said, giving him a pound.

Ice held his cell phone away from his ear and covered the speaker with his hand so whoever he was talking to couldn't hear what he was about to say. He kept his shit so tight only a select few knew all the things he was into. He knew. Dez knew. Until today, she thought she did, too, but if he was kicking it with JoJo without her catching wind of it, there was no telling what else she was in the dark about. "Make me proud," he said, sounding like the father she'd never had. "I'll see you out there."

"When do we find out who gets to go twice?" Bathsheba asked.

"Competitive. I like it. I won't make you wait too long, but don't get so hung up on impressing me you forget to handle your business." Ice put the cell phone back to his ear. "Hey, baby. I know you wanted to rent someplace upscale for your album release party, but I think we need to stay away from tuxes and black ties this time out. We should rent the Apollo instead. That way, we can show you're taking over New York but still keep it street. You can't try to be Jay-Z until you have his album sales."

"Forget his album sales," Raq said under her breath. "I'd rather have his wife."

"I heard that," Dez said. "Beyoncé's about as fine as my new whip."

"Your Navigator's righteous, but its curves can't compare with Mrs. Carter's."

"Beauty is in the eye of the beholder."

"Do you really think you're going to outdo me tonight?" Raq asked after everyone cleared out.

"I can dream, can't I?"

Raq didn't let Bathsheba's broad grin distract her from what was important. "Are you dreaming of trying to replace me, too, or just JoJo?"

Bathsheba's smile quickly faded. "I don't know what you mean."

"Are you sure about that? I've worked hard to establish my position. You're coming up behind me awful fast. Are you sure you aren't trying to use me to get ahead? All these questions you keep asking about Ice and his operation have me thinking you're trying to make some moves."

Bathsheba moved toward her. "What's gotten into you? I'm not trying to come between you and Ice, but, yes, I am using you."

"Say what?" Raq had hoped her instincts were wrong. She had hoped the voice in the back of her head that kept telling her she couldn't trust anyone but herself was wrong this time.

"I'm using every piece of advice you give me so I can become as good a fighter as you are."

Raq felt relief wash over her like water from a baptismal pool. "It's good to have a goal," she said with a laugh.

"You don't think I can reach it?"

Raq saw the determined look on Bathsheba's face and noted the defiant set of her jaw. "I think you can do anything you set your mind to."

"Including taking you out after we get paid? I don't want you to always be the one doing the asking."

Raq ran a fingertip across Bathsheba's cheek. Bathsheba's eyes grew wide at her touch. Raq watched the pupils darken as desire crossed Bathsheba's features. "It doesn't matter who's asking as long as the answer's yes, right?"

"You're a hard one to figure out."

"You're not trying to give up on me, are you?"

"I'm too stubborn to give up that easily." A knock on the door let them know it was time for Bathsheba to head to the ring. "Are you going to watch me fight?"

"I want to, but I don't want you looking at me when you should be keeping both eyes on your opponent. Remember everything we've been working on and you'll be fine. You can tell me all about it during the steak dinner you're going to buy me tomorrow night."

"Steak? I thought I was only going to be on the hook for a two-piece at Miss Marie's. After what you said at the Peking Gourmet, I thought you were a cheap date."

"Not when someone else is paying."

Bathsheba thought Raq was kidding about the steak dinner. A burger and fries seemed more her speed than a T-bone and a baked potato. But Bathsheba thought she might be on to something. If she took Raq to a steakhouse in downtown Baltimore instead of a cheap fast food joint in the Middle East, the change of scenery might shake her up enough to spill secrets she might not be willing to part with in the tight-knit confines of the 'hood.

She put her head down and headed to the ring. As an unknown commodity, she didn't know how the crowd would receive her. The lingering boos for Sabrina were so loud, they drowned out any cheers that might have greeted the announcement of her name.

She bounced on her toes as the referee recited the instructions. Sabrina had been animated as she taunted the crowd on her way to the ring, but she displayed a curious lack of energy as she stood flat-footed in the center of it.

"Who are you trying to be, the Energizer Bunny?"

Sabrina's voice sounded like a vinyl single being played at album speed. Bathsheba smelled weed on her breath and something astringent on her bandaged hands. Bathsheba would have to move like Keanu Reeves in *The Matrix* to make sure Sabrina's fists didn't get near her eyes.

"What's the matter?" Sabrina asked when Bathsheba didn't respond to her question. "Cat got your tongue?"

Bathsheba held up her fists. "In the ring, I like to do all my talking with these."

"Then let's chat."

As she headed to her corner to await the opening bell, Bathsheba told herself not to take Sabrina lightly. Though she had chemicals coursing through her body and slathered on it, she looked to be in pretty decent shape. Her record wasn't scintillating, but she had racked up enough wins to earn Bathsheba's respect.

When the bell rang, Bathsheba approached Sabrina warily. She slowly circled the ring as Sabrina stalked her, threw lazy jabs, and tried to draw her into a clinch so she could rake her knuckles across Bathsheba's eyes.

Bathsheba easily avoided both Sabrina's punches and her clumsy attempts at an embrace. The crowd began to whistle and yell for more action, but Bathsheba wasn't about to let them bait her into doing something stupid. She needed to stick to her game plan. The process might not be pretty, but she didn't care how she looked as long as she came away with the win. She could be flashy another day. If she lost, she might not get another fight. Then the entire investigation might be in jeopardy.

"That's it. That's the way," Zeke said, calling out encouragement from his seat in the audience. "Feel her out and find your rhythm."

Bathsheba nodded to indicate she had heard what he said. Zeke was such a good teacher. Unselfish, generous with his time, and eager to share his strategic acumen. He deserved to get hooked up with a boxer who possessed the talent and skills to succeed and a willingness to listen to someone who could help him maximize both. Raq could have been that boxer. If she managed to free herself from Ice's clutches, she still might be.

When the bell rang to end the round, Bathsheba felt the crowd getting restless. They were there to see a show. So far, she hadn't put on much of one. She thought she had landed enough punches to win the round on points, but the bloodthirsty crowd wanted to see knockouts, not decisions. She told herself to be patient, however, and wait for an opening instead of forcing the issue.

She got what she was looking for in the middle of the second round.

Sabrina missed with a wild right and left herself vulnerable. Bathsheba caught her on the chin with a left hook and sent her to the canvas. Bathsheba trotted to a neutral corner while the referee began his count. She wished he would hurry things along, but he seemed intent on taking his time.

When the count reached six, Sabrina pulled herself up on all fours and shook her head in an attempt to clear the cobwebs. At eight, she reached for the ring rope and tried to pull herself to her feet. She got halfway up before her legs gave out and she fell to her knees.

"Ten!"

The referee waved his arms and signaled that the fight was over.

Bathsheba felt both satisfaction and relief when she thrust her arms into the air. She hadn't been in the ring since her days at the academy. Though the circumstances had changed, the thrill of victory remained the same.

"I knew you had it in you," Raq said when Bathsheba made it back to the locker room, "but let me show you how it's done."

Raq's fight ended almost as soon as the opening bell rang. The first punch she threw was a devastating right that put her opponent to sleep. Her second fight, the one she contested in JoJo's absence, didn't last much longer.

Watching Raq in action, Bathsheba hoped she would never have to climb in the ring against her. Raq's superior height and reach would negate any advantages Bathsheba's speed might garner. And as for power, Raq had the edge there, too. If they ever found themselves at odds, Bathsheba didn't like her chances of winning.

"Everyone has a weakness," she said to herself as the main bout began. "Here's hoping I find hers before she finds mine."

CHAPTER ELEVEN

Raq was in a good mood. She had money in her pocket, food in her belly, a beautiful woman by her side, and the envy of all the people who had their eager faces pressed against the front window of Miss Marie's. The people on the outside couldn't see anything through the closed blinds, but that didn't stop them from trying. She had been in their position once. Now she was on the inside looking out instead of the outside trying to see in. She liked the view better from here.

Miss Marie's usually opened every morning at eleven, but it was almost noon and the doors were still locked. Raq and nearly a dozen members of Ice's crew occupied the booths and tables. No one looked like they planned to leave any time soon. If the staff didn't like it, they knew better than to complain. If they did, their asses would be on the street before they could get the words out.

Raq normally got her money and split so she could be out of sight by the time the judgmental church ladies started lining up for their after-service meals, but Bathsheba had convinced her to stick around. Raq was glad she had decided to give in. For the first time in years, she felt like she was part of a family.

She wiped her mouth with her paper napkin after she finished her lunch. The smothered pork chops she had ordered were so good she wanted to lick the gravy off the plate. As she leaned forward in her seat, she tapped her pocket with her fingers to make sure her pay envelope was still there.

Dez never announced how much everyone got paid when he handed out the cash each week, but Raq could tell by the thickness of the envelopes who the top earners were. Half Pint got a fat envelope each time out, but she was willing to put her take up against his any day. Especially this week. She was sitting on two or three thousand, easy. That second fight on Friday had put her over the top. JoJo's loss was her gain.

Instead of handing over most of her earnings to Zeke for safekeeping, she planned on holding on to all of this week's ducats herself. She'd need every one of them when she went to the Black Dahlia's album release party in New York. Ice had extended the invitation personally, and she planned to take him up on it.

She could hitch a ride with someone from the crew if she chipped in on gas money, but she didn't plan on sharing a hotel room with any of them when they arrived. She didn't know how much a hotel in New York would run her, but she doubted the reservation would come cheap. The expense would be worth it, though. She'd never been to the Big Apple before, and she wanted to see if it was everything everyone made it out to be. She didn't have enough scratch to make it rain in all of the clubs she and the crew would undoubtedly visit while they were there, but she had enough to get her through the weekend. And if Ice was footing the bill for the party, he would be popping bottles all night. High end or cheap, free liquor was free liquor.

Man. She couldn't wait to get the party started.

"Do you like rap music?" she asked.

Bathsheba stirred the melting ice in her orange soda with her straw. "Some of it. Not all."

"You like the Black Dahlia, though, right?"

"I've heard her stuff. Her beats are dope, but her rhymes need work."

"Whoa. Don't say that too loud." Raq looked around the room to see if anyone had heard. Thankfully, everyone else seemed to be too distracted by their hot meals and cold cash to pay attention to anything else. She lowered her voice in case someone was playing possum, spying on crewmates and ratting them out to Ice for a few extra bills in next week's envelope. There were few things she hated more than snitches. When you swore loyalty to someone, you weren't supposed to turn on them for love or money. "I'm not saying I don't agree with you, but you don't want to get caught saying something bad about Ice's girl."

"I hear you. Thanks for the heads-up. The Dahlia must have been who Ice was talking to on the phone before the fights Friday night. Did he really rent out the Apollo for her?"

"Yeah, and the party's going to be off the hook. Everybody who's anybody is going to be there. If you want to go, I can get you in."

Bathsheba seemed jazzed by the idea of being able to see celebrities in person instead of in a music video or in the movies. Her reaction made Raq feel important.

"I'd love to go, but I don't know if I'd be able to get off work. Since I'm a temp, I can't be asking for time off. I have a hard enough time making thirty hours as it is. I can't afford to give any of them away."

"Money isn't everything," Raq was surprised to hear herself say.

For her, money had been the be-all and end-all for as long as she could remember. Things were different now that her pockets were fat, but the knot she was sitting on now wouldn't last long. The trip to New York would take most of it. Then she'd be back to setting aside as much money as she could as she saved for a future she wasn't certain she would ever reach. Today, though, thoughts of the future paled in comparison with thoughts of the present. Thoughts of making Bathsheba happy. Seeing her smile. Watching her flash those dimples at everyone she met and being the lucky woman who got to take her home at the end of the night. That was worth any price she had to pay.

"Call in sick. Tell your supervisors you're coming down with something. What are they going to do, knock your door down to take your temperature and give you chicken soup if they find out you have a fever? No. They'll tell you to stay away as long as you can because they don't want to catch what you have."

Bathsheba smiled. "You have it all figured out, don't you?"

Raq felt her cheeks redden. "I just want to show you a good time, that's all. You trained hard, you won your first fight, and you're almost guaranteed to get another one. Now it's time to celebrate."

Bathsheba seemed impressed by all the things she had accomplished in so short a time. Raq certainly was. "Well. When you put it that way."

"So is that a yes?"

Bathsheba thought for a minute, which was fifty-nine seconds longer than Raq could stand. "Yeah, it's a yes."

"Sweet. I don't have any wheels. Do you mind if we take your car? I'll kick in on gas."

"You two sound like you're planning a road trip," Dez said. He was going table to table like a host checking in on guests he had invited to a dinner party. "Where are you thinking about going?"

"The Dahlia's party in New York. Ice invited me."

"When did he do that?"

"The day you came by the spot and said he wanted to see me."

Raq got a sinking feeling in her stomach as she stared into Dez's unsmiling face. Right on cue, Dez said, "Things have changed since then. Before you start making plans for the weekend, you'd better talk to Ice. I think he has a job for you."

"What kind of job?"

As he slid a toothpick from one side of his mouth to the other, Dez cut his eyes at Bathsheba like he didn't want to say too much in front of her. "You'll have to ask him."

"Is he in the office?"

"Yeah, but make sure you knock first. He had some calls to make, and I don't know if he's done."

"Why you acting like I'm a virgin all of a sudden?" Raq asked with a flash of anger. She crumpled her napkin in her fist to keep from lashing out in frustration. "I've been around long enough to know how shit works around here."

"Hey, don't bite my head off," Dez said, backing away. "I'm only the messenger."

Raq didn't know what she could say to convince Ice to change his mind, but she was certainly going to try. When she pushed her chair away from the table, Bathsheba rose as well.

"Do you need me to come with you?"

Raq had suspected Bathsheba was the type of person to have someone's back when they needed her. She looked around her. She had protected every person in this room at one time or another, but how many had come to her aid when she needed help? Just one. And she was staring her right in the face.

"Stay here. I'll be back in a few."

Bathsheba nodded and resumed her seat.

Raq tried to get her thoughts together as she headed down the narrow hall that led to Ice's office. She was glad Ice turned to her whenever he wanted a job done right, but she sometimes wished he'd find someone else he could depend on so she wouldn't have to be on call all the time. She liked having job security, but she hated not being able to live her life on her own terms. At her own pace. But if Ice did find someone else he trusted as much as he did her, she could go from sharing the load to not bearing any weight at all.

She felt silly by the time she knocked on the office door. She was in no position to make demands on someone like Ice. Not if she wanted to keep getting paid every week.

"Dez said you had a job for me?" she asked after Ice invited her inside.

"As a matter of fact, I do." Sitting behind a paperwork-strewn desk, Ice looked like any poindexter trying to make ends meet, but Raq knew better. He had so much money in the bank, he could probably live the rest of his life off nothing but the interest.

"What kind of job?"

"Close the door behind you and we'll talk about it."

Raq took a seat and waited for Ice to tell her what he needed done this time.

Ice laced his fingers on the pile of paper he had been sifting through. Behind him, a floor safe filled with neat stacks of crisp bills yawned open. There was probably more money in this room than the credit union up the street.

"Thank you for bringing Bathsheba to me. She's turning out to be everything you said she was."

Raq didn't let her head get too big because she could tell there was a "but" coming.

"But she seems too perfect to me. I need to make sure she isn't hiding something. I want you to check her out."

"I already did that. I followed her to her job like you asked me to. I watched the shop all day. All they're doing in there is making copies. There's nothing shady going on. She goes to work, she goes to the gym, and she goes home. That's it."

"I can see you believe she's on the up-and-up. But before *I* can be completely convinced, I need you to check out her place. I'll take her to New York this weekend so the record execs can have some eye candy to look at while we're doing business. While she's out of town, search her place to see what you can find."

"I don't know, Ice. If it's eye candy you need, why don't you take one of the pros? They get paid to be pretty."

"They get paid to suck dick, but that's not what I need this weekend." He scowled at her unexpected resistance. "Do I need to ask someone else to do this job?"

The thought of breaking into Bathsheba's apartment and invading her privacy made Raq uneasy, but she didn't want anyone else to take on the distasteful task. They might end up trashing the place instead of leaving it the way they had found it.

"I'm not trying to say I won't do the job—I'll do whatever you ask me to do—but what if Bathsheba doesn't leave town this weekend?"

"A free trip, all expenses paid? She'd be crazy to turn down an offer like that."

"We were planning to go to New York together. You invited me to the Dahlia's album release party, remember?" She waited for him to say the invitation still stood, but he remained ominously silent. "Bathsheba might not be willing to go without me," she said, feeling as lame as the excuse probably sounded.

"Perhaps not, but she doesn't have a choice."

From the look in Ice's eyes, Raq could tell she didn't have a choice, either.

"Call me when you finish the job," he said. "I want to know what you find the minute you find it, understand?" He leaned back in his swivel chair. "And don't worry about your girl. I'll make sure she never leaves my sight."

Ice's words offered cold comfort. Raq prayed her search of Bathsheba's apartment would come up empty. If it didn't, Bathsheba's trip to New York might be the last one she'd ever make.

"Is everything okay?" Bathsheba asked after Raq returned to the table.

Raq couldn't bring herself to meet Bathsheba's eye. "Everything's fine, but it looks like you'll be going to New York without me," she said, staring at the scarred tabletop.

"What kind of job does Ice have for you that's going to keep you tied up all weekend?"

"Nothing I can't handle." Raq finally looked up. "He's got one for you, too."

"For me?" Bathsheba couldn't hide her surprise. "What does he want me to do?"

"I wish I knew. He's waiting to see you in his office. If I were you, I wouldn't keep him waiting long."

❖

Bathsheba checked each of the bathroom stalls to make sure they were empty. Satisfied she was alone, she leaned over the sink and splashed cold water on her face as she tried to determine if she was about to move up or down. When she entered Ice's office, he would either offer her a promotion or set her up for a fall. She'd walk out with additional responsibility or get carried out with two bullets in her head.

She stared at her reflection in the mirror as excess water dripped from her chin.

"You're about to make this case or break it," she whispered. "What happens next is up to you."

She dried her face and hands, then threw the wadded-up paper towel in the trash. She wished she could toss her fears just as easily. She was about to come face-to-face with the most dangerous man in Baltimore, and she was armed with nothing but her wits and her instincts. She hoped they would be the only weapons she would need because they were the only ones she had.

She walked out of the bathroom and prepared to face her future, however short it might turn out to be.

"Come in. Come in," Ice said after she knocked on his office door.

Her gut told her his enthusiastic greeting was a cover for something, but she couldn't figure out what he was trying to hide. He didn't suspect her, did he? If he did, he'd be surrounded by armed guards waiting to follow orders instead of sitting here alone.

"How are things working out for you?" he asked with an ear-to-ear grin as she sat in the chair he indicated. The chair was hard gray metal, in sharp contrast to the sumptuous leather seat he occupied. "Is everyone treating you okay?"

She started to lie and give him the positive answer he probably expected, but remembering the scene in the locker room before the fight on Friday night, she decided to go in a different direction. "For the most part. JoJo hasn't welcomed me with open arms."

As she had hoped, Ice's smile faltered. His cheerful façade fell as his true nature came shining through. "The individual you just referenced has been excised from this organization. For all intents and purposes, she no longer exists. I thank you not to mention her name again. I don't like to repeat myself, so we will not be having this conversation again. Do I make myself clear?"

"Yes, sir." Bathsheba barked the words as if responding to a request from a superior officer.

"Yes, sir?" Ice asked with a chuckle and a mocking salute. "Are you military, ex-cop, or both?"

"Neither," Bathsheba said, desperately trying to patch the hole in her cover before it spread. "I don't look good in camouflage or navy blue."

Ice gave her an appraising look that made her long for a hot, cleansing shower. "I think you'd look good in just about anything—and even better in nothing at all."

Bathsheba fought to keep from rolling her eyes. She wondered if he'd used the same lines on JoJo and the Black Dahlia or if he'd saved his best ones for her. "Is that why you called me in here, to tell me to quit boxing and try my hand at one of your other business lines?"

He looked at her as if he didn't know what to make of her. If she could keep him off balance, she might have a chance to knock him off his perch once and for all.

"You did about as well as could be expected in your first fight," he said. "You got off to a slow start, but the exciting finish left the fans hungering for more. You could probably make some serious money in 'one of my other business lines,' as you put it, but people don't do well in that line of work without the right amount of desperation. You're more like Raq: hungry for things you don't have but willing to put in the work to earn them."

"My father always said there were three ways to go about getting the things you want. The right way, the wrong way, and the fast way. The wrong way and the fast way are usually one and the same."

"I assume your father took the right way?"

"No, he took the one that got him killed before he turned forty."

Ice blinked as if he'd just seen a vision of his own untimely end. "If you want to keep doing things your way," he said, clearing his throat to cover for his momentary loss of composure, "I don't anticipate having any problems finding a spot for you on an upcoming fight card."

"Upcoming? What about next week?"

"Friday's out of the question. It wouldn't do for your face to be marked up when I introduce you to my business associates in New York."

"Why me? I can't sing or rap. No amount of studio magic could disguise that."

"I don't need you to sing. I need you to talk. Unlike most of the knuckleheads around here, you seem to be able to string two sentences together without resorting to the colloquial or the profane. Like me, the people I'll be meeting with have vocabularies that aren't limited to 'fuck' and its various forms. I need someone who can carry on a conversation and look good doing it. I pick you."

"Thank you for thinking so highly of me, but I don't want to step on anyone's toes. Raq has been working for you a lot longer than I have. Why choose me instead of her?"

"Raq is a dedicated soldier, but she has, shall we say, very specific talents. Talents that might not suit my purposes in one venue but could be put to better use in another."

He sounded like a chess master dispassionately detailing game strategy. Except in his case, the pieces he was manipulating were human beings.

"Do you need an answer right away?" Bathsheba asked.

"I didn't hear myself ask a question."

Bathsheba squirmed in her seat to give Ice the idea his hard stare was making her nervous. "I'm supposed to work this Saturday. I can't take the day off without getting prior approval from my boss."

"If you do a good job this weekend, you won't have to worry about asking him for anything because the only person you'll be working for is me. You won't have benefits, but you don't have those now. Unlike minimum wage, my pay scale is something you could actually live on."

"What if I let you down?"

"That's a possibility neither of us wants to consider."

Threats and intimidation. Bathsheba was pretty sure Ice's leadership style didn't match those of the heads of Fortune 500 companies, but it seemed to work for him.

"I'll send a car to your place to pick you up first thing Saturday morning. The drive shouldn't take more than a few hours." He handed her several folded hundred dollar bills. "After you check into the hotel, buy yourself something nice to wear to the party."

Bathsheba unfolded the bills and fanned them out. "A thousand dollars?"

"You're going to be representing me this weekend. Buy yourself something that projects a professional image." He popped the collar on his crisply starched shirt. "Pretend you're me."

Something Raq and others like her had been doing for far too long. But if Bathsheba got her way, she would turn him from a role model into a cautionary tale. The person in the Middle East everyone wanted to emulate would become the convicted criminal no one wanted to be.

"See you next week," he said as she stood to leave.

"You can count on it."

CHAPTER TWELVE

Raq tugged the hood of her sweatshirt over her head as she watched the black town car pull away from the curb. Bathsheba had just climbed in the backseat and was now being driven to New York, a trip they had planned to take together until Ice's paranoia got in the way.

Raq didn't relish what she had been asked to do, but Ice was counting on her. As much as she wanted to, there was no way she could say no. She needed to force her way into Bathsheba's apartment, take a look around, and report what she found ASAP so Ice could realize what she already knew: that Bathsheba was on their side.

She needed to be fast, but she needed to be careful, too, or she might get caught in the act. Getting caught would fuck up Ice's plan by calling attention to it and ruin whatever she had going with Bathsheba. She didn't know if they were dating or just kicking it, but whatever it was felt good and she didn't want it to stop. A B&E charge would keep her off the streets for a few months, but Bathsheba might never forgive her for the betrayal.

"Focus," Raq said to herself, trying to get her mind right as she cased the scene.

People were everywhere, some putting a late end to their Friday night and others getting an early start on their Saturday morning. Raq couldn't do the job now. The block was too busy and Bathsheba hadn't been gone long enough. If she got it in her head she had left the stove on or something similar, she had time to ask the driver to make a U-turn so she could check the burner. With that in mind, Raq decided to wait until dark. There would be fewer people around and, by then, she'd be certain Bathsheba would be out of pocket for the weekend.

Raq went to Pop's to work off the anxiety most of her friends depended on weed to ease. Several hours later, after day had faded into night, she slipped out of the darkness and approached Bathsheba's apartment door. Even though the locks were new, Raq picked them in under two minutes. Not her fastest time, but it would do.

The latex gloves on her hands would prevent her from leaving fingerprints. The tight skullcap over her cornrows would prevent her from leaving DNA. She had watched *CSI* enough times to know how forensic investigators did their thing—and how to keep from leaving them what they were looking for.

She slipped the lock picks in her back pocket and took a quick look around before she let herself into the apartment. She didn't see anyone looking her way. Most people's attention was split between the dice game taking place on one end of the street and a territorial dispute between two homeless men wielding junk-filled shopping carts on the other.

Raq closed the door behind her and secured the locks that had given Bathsheba a false sense of security.

"Where to start?"

She had to be quick in case someone she hadn't noticed had called the cops, but she needed to be thorough so she could guarantee Ice her search results were accurate.

She started in the bedroom, the most obvious place for keeping secrets. She searched in the nightstand, in the dresser, in the closet, under the bed, and under the mattress, but she didn't find anything that wasn't supposed to be there.

A squat table lamp and battery-powered alarm clock sat on the nightstand. The standard-sized bed was neatly made. Raq made sure the cotton sheets and thick down comforter were as smooth as she had found them.

In the closet, blouses and pants hung on wooden hangers, the clothes arranged by color. Imagining how Bathsheba would look in some of the outfits, Raq ran her gloved hand over the rainbow of fabric. She visually checked out the small selection of tennis shoes, boots, and low-slung heels on the closet floor, then reached for the boxes lining the shelf. Instead of the shoes advertised on the outside, the boxes contained mementoes and souvenirs of a life Raq was able to piece together in less time than it had taken her to break into the apartment.

She headed to the small kitchen next. The cabinets were filled with the usual stuff. Canned goods, cereal, cleaning supplies, and pots and pans. The only thing she found interesting besides Bathsheba's endless supply of ramen noodles, was a Maxwell House can that contained cash instead of coffee grounds. Bills of various denominations were crammed inside the economy-sized tin. Mostly twenties, but ones, fives, tens, and a few fifties and hundreds, too. Whether it was rent money, a rainy day fund, or something else, Bathsheba was taking a chance having this kind of cash in her apartment. Anyone could find it if they knew where to look.

Raq put the can back where she had found it and made sure to turn the label in the same direction it had been facing so Bathsheba wouldn't notice the can had been moved. Then she headed to the living room, the last room she needed to clear before she could call Ice and tell him his instincts were wrong and hers were right on point. It wasn't often she got the chance to tell him I told you so, and she was looking forward to this one.

She searched the contents of the entertainment center first, opening each of the DVDs and CDs to make sure the disc inside matched the movie or album pictured on the box. After that tedious chore was done, she looked under the sofa cushions. She found fifty cents in loose change and a discarded condom wrapper that must have been left over from a previous tenant. When the cushions were back in place, she sat on the couch and sifted through the magazines spread in a semicircle on the coffee table. She learned all about Halle Berry's dream wedding to some French guy, the best ways to avoid temptation in the supermarket checkout line, and the latest athlete to go broke despite being paid millions during his career, but nothing incriminating was tucked between the magazines' glossy pages.

Enjoying the warmth inside the apartment a little while longer before she returned to the cold streets, she sat on the couch and pulled out her cell phone. Ice answered on the second ring. The sounds of loud music and even louder laughter greeted her before he did.

"Talk to me," he said eagerly.

"Like I told you before, she's clean. I searched her place from top to bottom, but I didn't find anything to make me doubt her."

"Good to hear. Where are you now?"

"Sitting on her living room sofa."

"Making yourself at home, huh?"

She was surprised she made him laugh, but the premium liquor he was probably swilling might have been the reason he was in such high spirits.

"I didn't think you wanted anyone to know what we were up to so I wanted to make sure I was alone."

"You thought right. I'm sure this assignment was difficult for you, but thanks for proving my faith in you isn't misplaced."

"You're welcome, Ice," she said, but the connection ended before she finished her sentence. "Call me any time. I'm sure you will anyway."

She leaned back on the sofa and folded her hands behind her head, taking satisfaction in her moral victory. Then she noticed one of the ceiling tiles bore a telltale stain. The kind of stain hands left behind after they had handled an object too many times.

"No matter how many times you wash your hands, the oil in your skin still rubs off."

She moved the magazines out of the way and stood on the coffee table, hoping she wouldn't have to call Ice back and tell him she was wrong. She lifted the tile with one hand and shoved the other into the opening.

"Shit," she said when her hand landed on two bulky objects laying side by side.

She shoved the tile aside and closed her eyes as pieces of particleboard rained on her head.

The first object was easy to identify even before she pulled it out of its leather holster. A snub-nosed .38 Special well oiled, fully loaded, and ready to fire. Raq wondered why

Bathsheba had stashed the gun in her ceiling instead of her nightstand. If someone busted in on her in the middle of the night, she wouldn't be able to get to the gun before they got to her.

Raq returned the gun to its hiding place and reached for the other object occupying the dark, cramped space. She pulled out a laptop computer. A name brand, not one of those no-name joints electronic stores sold for next to the nothing on the day after Thanksgiving. No wonder Bathsheba kept it hidden away.

Handling the computer with care, Raq set it on the coffee table, flipped it open, and hit the power button. Her hands began to sweat as she waited for the computer to fire up. If she found anything besides e-mails from and embarrassing photos taken by Bathsheba's former girlfriends, there would be hell to pay. And Raq would be footing part of the bill.

Raq prepared to search any files that might be saved on the computer's hard drive. She didn't see a printer anywhere. If she found anything of note, she'd have to take the computer with her so Ice could see what was on it for himself. Unless he trusted her enough to take her word for whatever she told him she'd discovered.

"Like that's going to happen. I already gave him the all clear. If I change my mind now, he'll never trust me again."

The computer chimed and the black screen turned blue. Raq leaned forward, her heart in her throat. Her heart nearly stopped when the computer prompted her to enter a password. How the fuck was she supposed to know what the password was?

She tried a few common phrases—Ravens, Baltimore, Charm City, Bathsheba, even Password—but nothing worked.

She had to stop before she locked the computer, but she couldn't stop until she found answers to the questions swirling in her mind.

Something was written below the password box on the screen. Raq leaned forward to read the tiny print.

"Password hint: The reason you're here."

Religious types were always saying Jesus was the reason for the season each Christmas so Raq typed that in, but it didn't work. She thought for a minute, then impulsively typed in Ice's name. If Bathsheba wanted to bring Ice down, he had to be the reason she was in the Middle East. Still no dice.

"Fuck."

She could keep guessing all day and never come up with the right answer. This was a job for Specs, the high school geek Ice kept on the payroll when he needed a computer network hacked or a code cracked. Specs could probably break through Bathsheba's defenses in less time than it had taken Raq to break into her apartment, but Raq wasn't ready to take it to that level yet. Not without proof Bathsheba was up to no good. Right now, she only had suspicions. In a court of law or in the streets, suspicions weren't enough. She needed more. One way or another, she intended to get it. Not for Ice's comfort but her own.

She turned the computer off, put it back where she'd found it, and lowered the ceiling tile into place. Then she cleaned the dust off the coffee table and arranged the magazines into a semicircle again. She experienced a brief moment of panic when she couldn't remember the order the magazines had been in when she entered the apartment, but there were so many of them she doubted Bathsheba would remember either.

She took one last look around. Satisfied she had left no sign she had ever been there, she unlocked the door and walked out.

Ice's questions had been answered, but hers were just beginning to form.

❖

The album release party had gone well—the Black Dahlia's songs had received rave reviews from the guests in attendance—but Bathsheba could feel the after-party begin to slide out of control. She didn't like the energy in the room. Angry, aggressive, and territorial.

Unlike at the Apollo, the guests in Roughneck weren't invited. The club was open to the public, which meant Ice's security team wasn't in charge of crowd control. Bathsheba wished she could talk to the people who were so she could find out what selection criteria they used when they decided who to let pass through the red velvet ropes. Only the women in the shortest, tightest outfits had been culled from the long line out front, along with the men who either dressed like thugs or carried themselves like them.

Bathsheba tensed each time someone neared the cordoned off VIP area where Ice was holding court. Ravenous eyes took in his, Dez's and the Black Dahlia's glittering jewelry and the endless supply of four-hundred-dollar per bottle champagne. Each time the cork on a fresh bottle popped and Ice or one of his crew shouted, "B-More, baby. Charm City in the house," the eyes watching the display grew a little narrower.

Bathsheba felt like she'd stumbled into a pissing contest between rival gangs. The posturing on both sides was harmless at the moment, but it might not remain that way for long. She could feel trouble brewing, though Ice appeared to be oblivious to the danger. He was too busy celebrating the Black Dahlia's success and, by extension, his own. He had been fairly subdued at the beginning of the evening—Bathsheba had chalked it up to nerves about how his first foray into the music business would be received—but he was positively jubilant now. Bathsheba replayed the evening in her mind to see if she could pinpoint the reason for the change in his demeanor.

She had arrived at the hotel shortly before eleven a.m. Her room hadn't been ready when she tried to check in, and the clerk wouldn't tell her if anyone else in her party had arrived so she had reluctantly left her overnight bag at the front desk and headed out on foot to select an outfit for the evening. It had taken her a while to find the right clothing store. The vintage and discount stores she had passed were ideal for her normal spending habits, but she had known they would never hold up to Ice's exacting standards. He preferred bespoke suits. She would love to own an outfit designed to fit her exact specifications, but she didn't want to pay four figures for the privilege.

On Malcolm X Boulevard, she had lucked upon a store that specialized in repurposing vintage fashions into modern styles. She had picked up a charcoal gray pinstriped suit, the masculine energy of which formed a perfect counterpoint to the pink blouse and black heels she had found on other racks in the same store. The entire outfit had cost about three hundred dollars, far less than the money Ice had allotted her. She had paid the bill with her credit card and made sure to ask for a receipt. When the case was over, she planned to submit an expense voucher for reimbursement. The money Ice had given her would be catalogued into evidence. Unlike the other women in his life, she wasn't for sale. Not at any price.

She adjusted the fit of the suit she had paid for with her own hard-earned money. Ice's reaction to seeing her in it had been positive but muted.

"You look ready to shine," he had said after giving her a slight nod of approval.

Even now, she wondered at the thrill that nod had provided. Was she so desperate for recognition she was willing to receive it from a man she considered her sworn enemy? She told herself she was excited because he was buying her cover, but part of her feared she might be falling prey to his considerable charm just like the other pawns on his chess board.

He had allegedly tasked her with entertaining the music industry executives in attendance at the Black Dahlia's album release party, but after it became clear the party was going to be a rousing success, he had been the perfect host, leaving her with little to do except offer the occasional rejoinder to a comment someone else made. Not that she minded. She learned more by observing than participating.

What she had observed at the Apollo had troubled her: Ice had spent as much time watching her as she had him.

She had caught him blatantly staring at her more than once, her skin prickling each time she had felt his eyes on her. For a moment, she had thought he suspected who she really was and what she sought to do. But after they arrived at Roughneck, the feeling had passed.

Ice had been noticeably tense when he answered a call on his cell. The ensuing conversation had taken place in a whisper despite the loud music and crowd noise in the background. Bathsheba hadn't been able to hear a word he said, and the club was too dark for her to be able to read his lips. Whatever the caller had told him seemed to please him, however. After he ended the call, he had been all smiles ever since.

"What's popping?" Dez had asked as a scantily dressed woman gyrated on his lap.

"This just officially became a night for celebration." Ice had raised a glass of champagne for a toast. Everyone else had followed suit, though Bathsheba's glass was filled with sparkling water instead of sparkling wine. Ice had arched an eyebrow. "You're not drinking, B?"

"Not when I'm in training," she had said, startled by his use of such a familiar term of address. *Or on a case.*

"Fuck that. One drink won't hurt. A night like this deserves a proper salute." He had snatched the glass from her hand, dumped the contents in a nearby ice bucket, and filled the glass with champagne. "That's more like it."

"What are we toasting to?" Dez had asked.

"To the Dahlia," Ice had said, draping an arm around the Black Dahlia's shoulders. "To Charm City showing New York how to run things."

Ice's flunkies had cheered so loud Ice hadn't seemed to notice the boos that had spread around the club like wildfire when the lead single off the Black Dahlia's album began to pump through the speakers. But Bathsheba had noticed them. She wished Ice would leave before the crowd completely turned on him, but he seemed too eager to flaunt his success.

"Let your haters be your motivators," he shouted, riling up the crowd even more.

His hubris could become his downfall. Perhaps not tonight, but eventually. Bathsheba would see to it—if someone else didn't do it first.

"Show them how it's done, baby."

Ice helped the Black Dahlia climb on a table. Tottering on eight-inch heels, she began rapping along to her own song, spitting the words with a mixture of pride and awe as if she couldn't believe she, a young woman from the projects of east Baltimore, was on the verge of mainstream success. Ice, Dez, and their bodyguards waved full glasses and half-empty bottles in the air like extras in a music video.

"Loosen up, B," Ice said, motioning for her to rise out of her seat. "This is a party, not a funeral."

Suddenly, it came close to being both.

One of the men who had been glaring at them for the past hour or so approached the VIP area with his right arm held low and tight to his body. Bathsheba didn't have to see the gun in his hand to know it was there. She reached for her own gun out of habit but came up empty. She armed herself with a champagne bottle, the only weapon at her disposal.

When the man raised his arm and yelled a testosterone-fueled insult, Bathsheba shouted, "Gun!" and smashed the champagne bottle against his wrist.

The gun bucked. A shot rang out. The bullet buried itself in the floor while Ice, Dez, and the Black Dahlia dove for cover. Patrons screamed in panic and began to rush for the doors. Ice and Dez's bodyguards, meanwhile, stood frozen in place, staring at the scene as if they wanted no part of it.

As the club descended into chaos, the man dropped his gun and cradled his right hand in his left. "Bitch, you broke my fucking wrist."

"Tough shit."

Bathsheba grabbed him by the collar of his oversized T-shirt, drove him to the ground, and held him in place by pressing her knee into the middle of his back. By the time the club's so-called security team showed up, she had the situation well in hand.

Ice peeked over the top of the velvet couch he had taken refuge behind. "Damn, girl. Raq must be training you right because you sure know how to kick some ass." His bodyguards laughed nervously. He turned on them immediately. "What are you slack-jawed motherfuckers laughing about? You allowed yourselves to be outdone by a female. How fucked up is that? I should fire you and put her in charge of security. Be glad I don't make you walk home."

"Calm down, man," Dez said, his voice echoing in the sudden silence. "You need to get out of here before the cops show up. Take everyone home. I'll stay here and clean up."

By "clean up," Bathsheba knew Dez meant he would grease the pockets of potential witnesses to make sure Ice's name wasn't connected to the incident. If the police called him in for questioning, it could be the beginning of the end of his criminal empire.

"I'll tell the driver to bring the limo around," Bigfoot said, trying to make himself useful.

Ice gave Dez a one-armed hug. "I'll see you back in Charm City, partner."

"Bet."

Ice's bodyguards circled him and the Black Dahlia as they made their way to the front door. A stretch limousine sat idling by the curb. Bigfoot opened one of the doors and ushered everyone inside.

The Black Dahlia was crying over the ignominious end to her big night. Ice offered her a few words of comfort before he stretched his hand toward Bathsheba. "I owe you my life. If it weren't for you, I wouldn't be sitting here right now."

Her feelings mixed, Bathsheba shook his proffered hand. When she had sensed danger, her police training had kicked in and she had acted on instinct without pausing to think. She had sworn to serve and protect. As the limousine sped toward the hotel, she wondered what would have happened if she had gone against her oath.

The man had been aiming for Ice's head. Would all her problems have been solved if she had allowed the shooter to take him out? Probably not. With Ice out of the picture, Dez would probably step into the void. It felt strange to say, but keeping Ice alive was the right thing to do. To ensure his empire fell, Bathsheba needed a conviction, not an execution.

CHAPTER THIRTEEN

News of Bathsheba's heroics made it back to the Middle East before she did. Raq couldn't go anywhere without hearing about how Bathsheba had stood up to a guy who had tried to pop Ice while Ice's so-called bodyguards cowered in fear. Rico, Hercules, and Bigfoot looked hard on the outside. On the inside, they were as soft as melting butter. Bathsheba was just the opposite. Even though she was all-girl, she could definitely hang with the boys.

Raq didn't know what to make of it. Ice had thought Bathsheba was keeping tabs on him, and Raq had found a hidden computer that might contain the proof Bathsheba was doing just that, yet Bathsheba had saved Ice's life by putting her own in danger. Raq didn't know anyone who would risk taking a bullet for someone they were gunning for themselves. If she had been standing next to someone she hated and some dude came charging at them like a rampaging bull, she would have shouted, "Olé!" as he passed by, not try to put herself between him and his target.

Whose side was Bathsheba on, Ice's or the cops'? Of all the questions swirling through Raq's mind, this one was easiest to answer. If Bathsheba was in Ice's corner, she wouldn't be acting like she had something to hide.

"We all have secrets," Pop loved to say. If that was the case, it was only a matter of time before Bathsheba's secrets came to light. When they did, Raq planned to be the one shining the spotlight on them. Then maybe Ice would realize he'd be better served by having her give orders instead of taking them. Ice and Dez might be the brains of the outfit, but she had ideas, too. All she needed was the right ammo to get Ice to take her seriously.

When people saw her, they thought she was all muscle. But she had a brain, too. And also, unfortunately, a heart. A heart that had started to warm to Bathsheba but was ready to turn cold in an instant. Loyalty was never-ending, but love had its limits. A lesson Raq had learned only too well.

She had never trusted her heart to anyone. Not after watching her friends give theirs away and get nothing but pain in return. Bathsheba had tempted her to go down that road, but she was glad she hadn't veered from her well-worn path. The route was lonely at times, but at least the ground beneath her feet was sure. She didn't have time for uncertainty. And Bathsheba was anything but a sure thing.

"That was pretty ballsy what you did," Zeke said as Bathsheba threw a flurry of punches at his padded hands. "What did Ice do to repay you?"

Raq, cooling down after spending thirty minutes on the speed bag, moved closer to the ring to hear Bathsheba's answer.

"Nothing." Bathsheba's eyes remained focused on her target as she threw a left-right-left combination. She continued to move forward as Zeke backpedaled, stalking him just like she would an actual opponent. Cutting off the angle, she pinned Zeke in a corner and unleashed a flurry of punches. Zeke was right. Bathsheba was rusty, but she had mad skills.

"He didn't have to pay me," she said, backing off to catch her breath, "because he doesn't owe me anything."

"He owes you his life," Raq said, resting her weary arms on the ring ropes. "Do you really expect anyone to believe he didn't offer you any kind of compensation in return?"

Bathsheba looked at her over her upraised gloves before she tucked her hands under her chin. "Just because someone offers you something doesn't mean you have to accept."

Raq couldn't tell if the comment was directed at her. It couldn't have been because the only things Ice had ever given her were money and respect. And they weren't given freely. She had put in the work to earn both.

"True that." Zeke adjusted the pads designed to protect his ribs from body shots. "Now Ice owes you a favor. Around here, that's worth more than a thank you any day. You have a fight this Friday night, right?"

"That's what they tell me."

"Then show me what you got."

Bathsheba tapped her gloves together, a sure sign she was loading up for a big right hand. Raq had picked up on the tell during Bathsheba's first fight. If Bathsheba didn't break the habit soon, other fighters might notice it, too, and devise a strategy to counter the punch. Raq already had one, but she wasn't about to share it. Not even with Bathsheba. In the ring, it was every woman for herself. Outside, it wasn't much different.

She looked around the gym. The room was filled with sweaty bodies learning the secrets of a dying art. Business was always steady, but it seemed to be picking up. Most of the boxers in the room were months behind on their weekly dues, but Zeke, like Pop before him, didn't have the heart to turn anyone away once they showed they were serious about making something of themselves.

"So I guess you're Ice's fair-haired girl these days, huh?" Raq asked after Bathsheba climbed out of the ring and another boxer took her place.

Bathsheba grabbed a water bottle and drained half of its contents before she answered Raq's question. "I wouldn't say that."

"What would you say?"

In court, people on trial were innocent until proven guilty. On the streets, the opposite was true. In her mind, Raq had already passed judgment on Bathsheba. The only thing left to do was hand out the sentence.

Bathsheba wiped her chin with the back of her hand while she gave Raq the same suspicious look Raq saw on her own face whenever she caught a glimpse of her reflection. "I'm saying it wouldn't feel right for me to jump ahead of you in Ice's crew. If anyone deserves to move up, it's you. You've put in the work. I'm just getting started. I'm willing to wait for my turn. It gives me more time to learn from the best. That's you, isn't it?"

"Some might say that."

Raq wasn't modest, but she wasn't one to brag, either. She slowly chewed a fingernail, an old habit she always reverted to in times of stress. Bathsheba seemed to have an answer for everything. Even though she said all the right things, did she really mean them?

"Are you ready for that steak?" Bathsheba asked as she unwound the protective tape on her hands. "I was thinking we could check out the restaurants downtown or along the Inner Harbor. I know a lot of tourists hang out there, but I hear the food's off the chain. What do you say?"

She smiled, showing off the dimples that always made Raq's stomach turn somersaults.

"No, thanks."

"What's the matter? Did you lose your appetite? I've seen you eat. I know that can't be the case."

"No chance of that."

Raq didn't go downtown unless she was low on cash and she was looking for pockets to pick. Even then, she didn't stay long. She chose her marks, fleeced them, and hit the nearest pawnshop before her victims realized they had been robbed. But it wasn't the proposed venue that gave her pause. It was the person inviting her to it. A week ago, she would have loved nothing more than having a fancy sit-down dinner with Bathsheba. Getting cleaned up nice and watching people's mouths drop when she walked in with Bathsheba on her arm. Now, though, she didn't think she could stomach it, no matter how good the food.

"Save your money," she said. "There's no reason for you to drop three figures on a meal we could make ourselves for twenty bucks."

"Then let's make it ourselves."

Raq snorted a laugh. "Who's going to do the cooking, me or you? I hope you don't expect me to do it because my culinary skills are limited to things that come out of a can or go in the microwave. Unless you want your steak to taste like charcoal or shoe leather, you don't want me in the kitchen."

"No, I don't want you in my kitchen," Bathsheba said with a laugh of her own.

"See? I told you."

Raq felt herself begin to loosen up a bit. She hadn't been able to relax around Bathsheba since Bathsheba had come back to town. She didn't want Bathsheba to know she suspected she was being less than honest about who she was and what she was doing in the Middle East, but she couldn't convince herself to act like nothing had changed. Like she hadn't seen what she'd seen in Bathsheba's apartment. Like Bathsheba was no longer a friend but an enemy. An enemy she needed to deal with, one way or another. Ice's way would be more permanent; hers would cause more pain. Pain was something she knew well. How to take it and especially how to dish it out.

Bathsheba moved toward her. "I don't want you in my kitchen because I'd rather have you in my bed." She trailed her fingers down Raq's arm, leaving sparks in their wake. She was standing so close Raq could feel her breath kiss her skin. Raq forced herself to stand her ground. To stand firm. Hard to do when she knew how easy it would be to give in. "My place tonight at eight. How does that sound?"

Raq's clit twitched as desire raced through her like a wildfire. Her head told her Bathsheba was bad news—that Ice was right not to trust her—but her heart said something different. Her heart begged her to take a chance. To allow what she and Bathsheba had started to reach its natural conclusion, regardless of outside influences. But she refused to listen. Unlike Ice, she wasn't going to let herself be distracted by a pretty face. Not when there was work to be done. And truth to be discovered.

When they first met, Bathsheba had played hard to get. She had made a big deal about Raq earning the crumbs she threw out. Now she was offering to give her cookies away after one night at the club and a couple of lunch dates? It didn't add up. Unless she was trying to throw Raq off the scent by tossing a little sex her way. Could Bathsheba tell Raq had doubts about her? Of course she could. Even Stevie Wonder could see that.

Raq wasn't doing a good job of hiding her suspicions, if Bathsheba's guarded expression was any indication. The way she saw it, there were two things she could do: confront Bathsheba head-on with what she had found or sit back and wait for her to trip herself up. There were problems with both. If she asked Bathsheba about the computer, she'd have to explain how she knew about it in the first place. And if she waited, there was no telling what kind of damage Bathsheba could do to Ice and his organization in the meantime. Waiting could put her out of a job, behind bars, or both. She didn't like either prospect.

She had to find out what Bathsheba was up to without letting Bathsheba know she had broken into her place and without Ice finding out she had kept her initial discovery from him. Guaranteed to lose either the respect of a man she looked up to or the affections of a woman she was beginning to care for, she was fucked either way.

There was only one person she could turn to for help. Pop Walker. The man who had saved her years ago could do the same now.

Pop was one of the oldest residents of the Middle East. He had watched multiple generations grow up before his eyes and could dish the dirt on all of them. Bathsheba had said she had lived in the Middle East all her life, but Raq had never seen her around. If Bathsheba was lying about her past—or anything else—Pop would know. He and Raq weren't as close as they used to be, thanks to her dealings with Ice, but she knew she could always count on him to give her the straight dope.

"I can't come to your place tonight."

"Why not?" The look of disappointment on Bathsheba's face seemed so genuine Raq almost forgot she might be acting. "Do you have to work?"

"No. I'm supposed to eat at Pop and Zeke's place tonight. It's something we do every week." At least they used to before she started working for Ice. But Raq didn't think it would take much work on her part to convince Pop and Zeke to turn back the clock and reestablish their old tradition. "Would you like to join us? Pop and Zeke don't get much company. It's just the two of them most nights. I think they'd enjoy having someone to talk to besides me."

"I'd like that."

Bathsheba's smile was tinged with relief, an emotion Raq doubted she would feel any time soon. All she expected to feel for the foreseeable future was regret.

"Cool. Pop and Zeke live above the gym, so we won't have far to go. I'll meet you here at seven."

And if Pop was his usual nosy self, Raq would know everything there was to know about Bathsheba Morris by nine.

❖

The signs were subtle, but Bathsheba could tell Raq suspected she was something other than what she was pretending to be. She had known as soon as she'd walked into her living room and noticed the magazines on her coffee table were in a different order than she'd left them. That her gun, instead of pointing north and south, was directed east and west. Everything else, including her computer, was in place, if not undisturbed, but she had been able to tell someone had been in her apartment. Not someone. Raq.

Bathsheba was the reason Raq had been asked to stay behind when Ice and his inner circle went to New York. She had done something to raise Ice's suspicions and, just like at the copy shop, he had sent Raq to her apartment to check her out. Though Ice's concerns had been assuaged, Raq's obviously had not. Tellingly, Raq had kept her reservations to herself instead of sharing them with Ice. If Raq had confided in him, Bathsheba would be sitting in front of him refuting Raq's claims or pleading for her life, not planning a dinner date.

Unless Raq had guessed the password to her computer, which was a long shot but not impossible, she wouldn't have been able to gain access to the files stored on the hard drive. Which meant that odds were in Bathsheba's favor. Raq didn't know she was a cop. Good. Bathsheba had time to win her over before she lost her altogether.

She picked out an outfit that was sexy without being too obvious—tight jeans that fit her like a second skin and a lavender silk blouse that was one button away from being extraneous. Raq's eyes bugged out when she saw her, letting Bathsheba know she had chosen wisely.

"I hope you like seafood," Raq said after she regained her composure. "Zeke told me he was making a pot of Maryland blue crabs. When he seasons them just right, they're so good they make you want to slap your mama."

Bathsheba had felt like doing that every day since she was a teenager, but she didn't feel like sharing that part of her life with anyone, though she knew she might have to at some point for the sake of the case.

"It's been a while since I've had homemade blue crabs."

In truth, it had been a while since she'd had homemade anything. When she walked a beat, she and her partner used to hit the same diner so often the waitress had their orders ready even before they walked in the door. When she rode in a patrol car, fast food places were her best friends. After she became a detective, she learned to live on day-old coffee and leftover pizza. Now that she was undercover, she was more focused on solving the case than finding her next meal.

"Then you're in for a treat." Raq opened the door for her and gallantly stepped aside. "After you."

Bathsheba's heart hammered in her chest as she stepped inside the darkened gym. She didn't like having someone on her six, especially when she didn't know if it was someone she could trust. She slowed so Raq could draw ahead of her instead of trailing behind.

"Pop and Zeke's apartment is this way."

Raq pointed across the room toward a set of narrow stairs behind a small practice ring. The wood on the oak railings was worn smooth from use. Bathsheba let her fingers slide across the railings' shiny surface as she followed Raq up the stairs. Word on the street was Raq never carried a gun, but that didn't stop Bathsheba from performing a quick visual inspection to make sure.

Raq's jeans and hooded sweatshirt were loose, as was her norm, but Bathsheba didn't see any telltale bulges under the voluminous material that would indicate she was hiding a concealed weapon. Raq might not be leading her into an ambush, but she definitely seemed to have something in mind besides food and fellowship.

As Bathsheba passed a tapestry of the Last Supper in the foyer, she hoped she wasn't about to attend her own version of one.

The apartment smelled like an extension of the gym—the aromas of sweat and various balms meant to treat sore muscles permeated the small space. Pop Walker sat in a faux leather armchair whose seat had molded over time to fit his shrunken form.

Pop was in his nineties now and he had been a senior citizen for as long as Bathsheba had known him, but she remembered when he was the biggest, baddest man on the block. Though he was slight in stature, the sculpted muscles that were holdovers from his days in the ring had made him appear larger than life even in his sixties. How things had changed. Pop, a shell of his former self, was locked in a losing battle against the one opponent who was destined to remain undefeated: time.

"It's good to see you, Raquel."

Raq glanced back at Bathsheba as Pop opened his arms for a hug. His warm greeting confirmed Bathsheba's suspicions that tonight's dinner was more of a ruse than a ritual.

"Does your presence tonight mean what I think it means?" Pop asked.

"No. I just—" Raq shifted from one foot to the other. She looked like she had disappointed someone she longed to impress. "I just missed you, that's all. I was hoping we could put the recent past behind us and go back to the way it used to be. At least for one night."

Raq rubbed the back of her neck as if she were embarrassed by having her emotions on display. Bathsheba found the move oddly endearing—and utterly captivating. One of Raq's duties was to provide protection for drug dealers as they plied their trade. At the moment, however, she seemed to need looking after far more than they ever did. Bathsheba wanted to go to her and offer comfort, but Pop made the move before she could.

"Yeah, baby girl," Pop said, taking one of Raq's large hands in his smaller one. "We can do that. You brought company, I see."

"I'd like you to meet Bathsheba Morris."

Bathsheba stepped forward to shake Pop's outstretched hand.

"I thought you got out." He looked her in the eye as he gripped her hand hard. As if he wanted to tell her something he couldn't say in words. "What are you doing back here?"

"You know her?" Raq asked.

"Are you serious? Of course I know her. I watched her grow up the same as I did you." He turned back to Bathsheba. "How's your sister doing? Did she get herself sorted out?"

Bathsheba felt an all-too-familiar disappointment. "Mary's trying, but it's hard, you know?"

"I know." Pop patted her hand soothingly and released his hold. "Once that narcotic gets hold of you, it doesn't want to let go. I've seen it plenty of times but never experienced it firsthand, thank the Lord. Did you come back to try to save your mama like you did your sister?"

An unexpected lump formed in Bathsheba's throat. The only emotion she usually felt for her mother was anger, not empathy. "I've done all I can do. I can't save someone who doesn't want to be saved."

"She wants help. She just doesn't know it yet. She has to hit rock bottom first."

"I've heard what she does just to get another hit," Bathsheba said. "She's already at rock bottom."

"Does your mama live around here?" Raq asked. "What's her name?"

"Ask your friend Half Pint," Pop said contemptuously. "He can tell you everything you need to know."

Raq shook her head as if she wanted to contest Pop's statement, then her mouth fell open in obvious recognition. Her haunted eyes made it clear she wished she could recast her role in the tragedy playing out around them. "Gumby's your mama?"

"Her name isn't Gumby," Bathsheba said with a flash of heat. "It's Delilah."

"Sorry. I didn't mean any offense." Raq slowly lifted her broad shoulders in a shrug. "I figured she was somebody's mama, but I didn't know she was yours."

"Would it have made a difference?"

"If I'd known she was your people, yeah."

"And what would you have done?"

"I would have stepped in and put a stop to the things Half Pint was making her do."

"Delilah had to have some kind of connection to you in order for you to be willing to do something to keep her from being degraded?" Pop asked. "Finding out she's Bathsheba's mother shouldn't be the reason you developed a conscience. You should have seen a person in trouble and lent a hand no matter what. Now that you know who she is, what are you going to do about it, help her out or keep looking the other way?"

Raq shrank from the tongue lashing. "I do what I'm told," she said defensively.

"I remember when you used to have a mind of your own," Pop said. "It hasn't been that long since you were able to think for yourself, has it?"

Raq clenched and unclenched her fists as if she wanted to hit something to release her growing frustration at being trapped between the world she once knew and the one in which she had chosen to live. "I thought we said we weren't going to talk about this tonight."

"My house. My rules," Pop said sternly. Then he quickly relented, his soft spot for Raq preventing him from causing her more discomfort. "You're right. I don't want to ruin my appetite before dinner by dwelling on unpleasant subjects." He jerked his head toward the kitchen. "Why don't you go check on Zeke and make sure he puts enough mustard in the potato salad?"

Raq was so happy to leave the unpleasant scene behind she ran to the kitchen as if someone was chasing her.

"Since Zeke's in charge of the crabs and Raq's taking care of the potato salad, what would you like me to do?" Bathsheba asked.

Pop took a quick glance toward the kitchen, where Zeke and Raq were banging pots and pans like they were in the percussion section of a marching band. "I know you're a cop," Pop said in a whisper.

Bathsheba tried to remain calm despite the rush of adrenaline and fear that surged through her. "Why would I want to be a cop?" she asked in an attempt at levity. "They get lousy pay, terrible benefits, and people don't appreciate them until they need one. Sometimes not even then."

"I saw your picture in the paper when you busted some wannabe gangbangers in DC a few years back."

Bathsheba remembered the article and the grainy photo that had accompanied it. Something that had once been a point of pride could turn out to be the bane of her existence if the wrong person got wind of it.

"Do you want me to call you Bathsheba or Renee? Renee's the name you really go by, isn't it?"

"Bathsheba's fine," she said after making sure Raq and Zeke were out of earshot. Pop seemed to be on her side, but she wondered if he represented the minority or the majority. "How many people have you told I'm a cop?"

"I know how things are around here. Ice Taylor has bought everyone's silence or their cooperation. The only questions they're willing to answer are the ones he asks. I haven't said a word to anyone, including Zeke. I don't want him to be compromised by having access to information he might not need."

"So what do you want from me?"

"I want you to say the real reason you came back to the Middle East is to take Ice Taylor down. If it is, have a seat and tell me what I can do to help."

"I can't ask you to put yourself at risk."

"You're not asking. I'm volunteering. It seems to me you don't have much choice. You're in enemy territory, Bathsheba, and you need as many allies as you can get."

"No," Bathsheba said. "All I need is one."

❖

Raq munched on a carrot stick while she watched Bathsheba and Pop sit and talk like she and Pop used to do. Instead of jealous, she felt confused. And stupid. Bathsheba wasn't a cop. She was just like her. A normal, everyday person with normal, everyday problems and enough family drama to supply the soap operas she loved to watch with plot lines for years to come.

"Did you know Gumby was Bathsheba's mama?"

"No." Sweat poured down Zeke's face as he leaned over a giant pot of blue crabs. "But now that you mention it, I can definitely see the family resemblance."

Raq mentally compared Gumby's and Bathsheba's faces. One was haggard and deeply lined. The other was as smooth and beautiful as a piece of polished mahogany. But they had the same almond-shaped eyes, the same pert nose, and the same full, sensuous lips. Of course they did. Because the faces belonged to mother and daughter.

"How could I not have noticed it before?"

Zeke stuck a fork in a bobbing ear of corn to see if the kernels were tender enough to eat. "Maybe you did and you didn't want to accept what you were seeing."

"Either way, I owe Bathsheba an apology."

"For what? For not trying to save her mother from her demons?"

"No, for thinking she was a cop." Raq waved her hand in front of her face after Zeke poured the pot of blue crabs, corn on the cob, and the accompanying hot water in an oversized colander in the sink and thick clouds of steam filled the small kitchen.

"Damn, girl. Why would you think that?" Zeke wiped his dripping face with a dish towel. "I mean take a look around. Ain't no cops hanging around the Middle East. They don't even come when called, let alone volunteer to stay here full-time."

"They would if they were undercover."

"How long do you think undercover cops would last on these streets? Someone would roll over on them the day they showed up. Both them and their half-assed cover stories would get shot to hell. Boom. End of investigation."

"That's what worries me."

She followed Zeke to the patio, where he spread butcher paper on a rectangular table and dumped the corn and blue crabs on top.

"What do you mean?" Zeke asked as he set the table.

Raq placed a bowl of potato salad on one end of the table and a container of cole slaw on the other. "I'm not the only one who had doubts about her. If someone acts on theirs instead of clearing them up like I did, boom. End of Bathsheba."

"Then do what you do best: protect the ones you love."

For Raq, that was easier said than done. Whose side was she supposed to take when the ones she loved needed protection from each other? As she watched Pop slowly walk toward the patio while leaning on Bathsheba's arm for support, the choice became clearer.

"When this is over, can we go back to my place?" Raq pulled out Bathsheba's chair and sat across the table from her. "There's something I want to show you."

"Something like what?" Bathsheba asked, spreading a napkin in her lap.

"Me."

CHAPTER FOURTEEN

Raq unlocked her apartment door, flipped on the lights, and tossed her keys on top of the collected spare change in the plastic pretzel jar next to the miniscule TV. The three-gallon jar was bigger than the TV set. Hell. It was practically bigger than the entire apartment. She could probably score roomier digs if she filled out the right paperwork with the pencil pushers in DC, but who had time for that? The place was small—room enough for a bed, bathroom, and "kitchen," an area she had carved out for a hot pot and a small refrigerator—but it had all the space she needed. Until now. Having Bathsheba here made her realize how little she had. And how much she wanted.

"This is me. It's not much, but it's mine."

"Cool."

Bathsheba looked around, which took all of two seconds since the place was less than four hundred square feet. Raq was glad she had made her bed this morning, something she didn't normally do unless she was expecting company. Inviting Bathsheba home with her after dinner with Pop and Zeke hadn't been part of the original plan at the beginning of the night. Now she couldn't think of a better way to end it.

"Can I get you something to drink?" Raq bent to check the contents of her mini-fridge. "I've got soda, juice, water. Check that. Looks like the juice expired last week. You don't want that." She pulled the expired carton of OJ out of the fridge so she could toss it in the trash. "I thought I had some beer, but I guess I polished it off already. You don't strike me as an Olde English kind of girl anyway. Next time you come over, I'll be sure to have a bottle of wine on hand. The good stuff, not Night Train. You could light fires with that shit. So what would you like?"

"For you to stop trying so hard." Bathsheba held Raq by her shoulders, grounding her when she felt like she might fly away. "Stop trying to impress me and just be real with me. That's all I've ever wanted from you. Nothing more. Nothing less. If you invited me here to help you clean out your refrigerator, grab a trash bag and let's get to it. But if you had something more serious on the agenda, I'd rather get to that instead."

Accepting Bathsheba's challenge, Raq grabbed two bottles of water out of the refrigerator, took Bathsheba by the hand, and led her to a nearby chair. "First of all, I want to tell you I'm sorry. I didn't know Gum—I mean Delilah—was your mother. Now that I know who she is, I promise I'll do my best to keep her safe. She's one of Half Pint's best customers so he won't want to hear it when I tell him he has to drop her, but I don't think it will take much persuading on my part to get him to see things my way."

"I appreciate that. Thank you."

Raq didn't know how Ice would react to her messing with his bottom line—he kept track of every penny that went in and out of his organization—but she'd deal with that situation when the time came.

She placed her unopened bottle of water on the floor, sat back in her chair, and rubbed her hands over the creases in her jeans. She felt as nervous as a whore in church. She had bared her flesh before but never her soul. Tonight, that was going to change.

"Knowing where you come from answers a lot of questions I had about you," she said.

"What kind of questions?"

Bathsheba sounded tense so Raq put a hand on her knee to get her to relax. "Like why you've kept the things in your past such a big secret. Before tonight, I thought you'd told me everything there was to know about you. Now I realize I don't know as much as I thought I did. If Pop hadn't said something tonight, would you have told me about your sister and your Mom?"

"Eventually." Bathsheba took a sip of her water as she tried to buy time. Then she set the bottle down and stared at her feet. "If I thought we were going to get serious, yes, I would have told you everything."

"*If?* You don't think I'm serious about you?" Raq put her fingers under Bathsheba's chin and tilted her head up until Bathsheba met her eyes. "That's why I brought you here tonight. Because I wanted to let you know how much you mean to me. Because I wanted to introduce you to the real me."

Bathsheba leaned forward in her seat, giving Raq her full, undivided attention. "Good. Because I'm ready to meet her."

Raq cleared her throat, reluctant to tell her tale but eager for Bathsheba to hear it. She had glossed over it the night they went to Club Peaches, but now it was time for her to spill the whole T.

"When I was fifteen, my Mom's boyfriend, Ray, started looking at me like he hadn't eaten in a week and I was a bucket of KFC. He didn't do anything at first. Then he started hinting around and asking me questions to see if I was interested. I came out of the womb liking girls so he knew the answer was no. He tried to beat the gay out of me, but that didn't work, either. Then he decided to take what I wouldn't give him. I'd started going to Pop's Gym the first time Ray looked at me sideways. I wanted to be able to defend myself without reaching for a knife or a gun. I didn't want to exchange one prison for another."

"Did you tell your mother what was happening or did she turn a blind eye to what was going on?"

"She convinced herself my bruises came from fights at school. I tried to tell her the truth, but she accused me of trying to seduce Ray when it was the other way around. She was passed out drunk the night he finally made his move. I woke up with him on top of me, pinning me down, and trying to pull my underwear aside so he could shove his way inside."

Bathsheba sat on the edge of her seat like she was watching an action movie. "What did you do?"

"I slammed my knee into his balls as hard as I could. A cheap shot, maybe, but it slowed him down long enough for me to free my hands. Once we were on even terms, he didn't have a chance. I knocked him out with a right cross. The purest punch I've ever thrown. While he slept off the effects of the punch and the forty of malt liquor he and my mother had split, I packed my shit and got out."

"And you went to Pop's?"

Raq nodded. "I stayed with him and Zeke for almost three years. Pop probably would have let me stay indefinitely if I asked, but he was on a fixed income and I knew how much of a strain it put on him to have another mouth to feed. I needed to find a job so I could pull my weight. I tried the minimum wage thing for a while, but the take-home pay was so bad it was like I was working for free. I got tired of giving most of my money to the government each week. Then Ice came along. He offered me two things: more money and the chance to do what I do best, box. I would have jumped ship for either one, but he offered me both."

"What did he ask you to do for him?"

"He wanted me to sell for him because I knew how to handle myself and he didn't think any of the rival crews would try to jack me for my cash or my stash. But I said no. I don't care how other people make their living. That's on them. But there are two things I will never do, no matter how much someone offered to pay me: sling drugs or carry a gun."

"Yet you look out for people that do. What's the difference?"

"Everyone needs someone to watch his back from time to time. What I do isn't illegal. To me, it's just a job like any other. But not everyone sees it that way."

"You mean Pop."

"He's not the only one who doesn't like what I do. He's just the most vocal about it. He doesn't approve of the drug thing, but I think the unlicensed boxing upsets him even more."

"Why? He's the one who introduced you to the sport in the first place."

"That's why he's so hurt. He wanted me to fight in the Golden Gloves or the Olympics, not warehouses and back alleys."

"Wouldn't you have preferred to take that route?"

Raq ran her hand over her cornrows, wondering if the disappointment she sometimes felt after a particularly lopsided win was hers or someone else's. If she fought in a different venue, the reward might have been greater, but the cheers would have sounded the same and the stakes wouldn't have been nearly as high. "Those were Pop's dreams, not mine."

"What do you dream about?"

"Leaving here." Raq let her hands fall into her lap, thankful for the change in subject. "Going someplace far, far away. Somewhere I could have room to breathe. Someplace I wouldn't have to look over my shoulder all the time because no one's out to get me. Someplace quiet with no gunshots or police sirens ripping through the night."

"Sounds like heaven."

Raq raised her bottle of water in a toast. "Here's hoping I don't have to die to get there."

"I hope you don't either. I like having you here." Bathsheba covered Raq's hand with hers. "When you find the slice of heaven you've been dreaming about, maybe I could visit you sometime."

Raq laced her fingers through Bathsheba's, forming a connection like she had never felt. "Or maybe you could come with me."

"Do you want me with you?"

Raq slid out of her chair and knelt before Bathsheba. "With everything I am, yes, I want you."

Bathsheba cradled Raq's head in her arms, taking her from the Middle East to a place that had previously existed only in her imagination. She didn't have to die to go to heaven because she was already there. She closed her eyes, feeling safe. Feeling secure. Feeling loved. Feeling some things she hadn't felt in years and something she had never felt before. She wanted to explore those feelings. To see how deep they were. To see how much further they could go.

She lifted her head, hoping she had done enough to earn the kiss she was silently requesting. Bathsheba lowered her head until their mouths met in a kiss so tender it nearly brought tears to Raq's eyes.

Raq slid her hands under Bathsheba's blouse as the kiss deepened, needing to feel her skin. Needing to feel her heart. Bathsheba pulled at Raq's hoodie and Raq lifted her arms to comply. She needed Bathsheba's hands on her, too.

But her phone rang before she could get what she had craved for weeks.

"Hold that thought," she said as she dug her burner out of her pocket.

"It's me." Ice's controlled, measured voice cooled Raq's raging libido. And the fact that he sounded like himself instead of a Denzel wannabe garnered her immediate attention.

"What's up? Is something wrong?"

Something had to be screwed up somewhere. Otherwise, Dez would be calling. If Ice was reaching out, the shit must have really hit the fan.

"I'll tell you when you get here. Meet me at the storage unit. And bring Bathsheba with you."

"Why?" she asked, but Ice didn't answer because he had already hung up.

The knot of apprehension in Raq's stomach grew even tighter after she told Bathsheba they had to leave.

"Why does he want me to come?"

Raq doubted Bathsheba knew anything about the self-storage company Ice owned, what most of the units contained, or the kinds of things that went on in the large, empty unit on the far end of the lot. But she may be about to find out.

"I don't know, but it sounds like we have work to do."

❖

Island Blue Self-Storage was located on the outskirts of Baltimore, a short drive from the heart of town in one direction and the docks in another. Members of the drug enforcement squad had sat on the units for hours on end but had never witnessed any criminal activity taking place on the premises of the vast site. Just the usual comings and goings of regular paying customers moving their belongings into or out of the storage spaces as needed. The drug squad had deemed Island Blue one of Ice's legitimate businesses and it had quickly fallen off the radar as attention turned to Miss Marie's instead.

The drug squad, Bathsheba decided as she watched bricks of cocaine being secured behind a unit's locked door, obviously hadn't looked hard enough. Ice's supply wasn't sitting in some warehouse the police hadn't been able to locate but in dozens of storage units they had chosen to ignore. Millions of dollars hiding practically in plain sight.

Bathsheba needed to get word to Carswell so he could set up round-the-clock surveillance. She still didn't have enough evidence to take Ice down—she needed to prove the coke belonged to him instead of a rent-paying customer—but she had just taken a large step toward cracking the case. She was so close now she could almost see the finish line. But instead of jubilation, she felt only trepidation.

There was a reason she had been brought here. A reason she was being allowed to see what she was seeing. Either

Ice trusted her enough to show her the inner workings of his organization or she wouldn't be allowed to live long enough to tell anyone what she had seen.

Bigfoot and Winky stood outside a large unit on the end of the lot. When he saw Bathsheba and Raq approach, Bigfoot bent and lifted the unit's retractable door. Light spilled out from the unit's interior, mingling with the harsh glow emanating from the security lights overhead.

"Go on in," Bigfoot said. "They're waiting for you."

Bathsheba and Raq ducked under the half-open door. Bathsheba tried not to flinch when the door slammed shut behind them.

Ice, flanked by Dez and One-Eyed Mike, stood at the front of the unit. Before him sat a small figure bound to a chair. The figure's face bore little resemblance to the mug shots and surveillance photos Bathsheba had seen. Half Pint's once-handsome face was grotesquely swollen, the results of what must have been a savage beating.

"You're here," Ice said, puffing on a cigar. "Now we can get this party started."

"Get it started?" Raq said. "It looks like it's almost over. What have I missed?"

"It seems Rashad has forgotten who calls the shots around here. He's forgotten that I have eyes everywhere. I run the streets of Charm City, not some little boy pretending to be a man."

Half Pint whimpered and fiercely shook his head from side to side, the bloody gag in his mouth preventing him from verbally proclaiming his innocence. Tears ran down his ravaged cheeks, even though one eye was bloodshot and the other was swollen shut.

"Did you know he was planning to go into business on his own?" Ice asked. "That he was siphoning off kilos of my product to build a stash of his own?"

"No," Raq said. "You pay me to watch him when he's on the streets, but I'm not with him twenty-four seven."

"So you do think he's capable of betraying me?"

"All I've ever heard him say is how much he wanted—*wants* to be like you. He said the two of you were tight."

"He said a lot of things. But tonight's the last night he'll ever use my name in vain." Using a handkerchief to mask his fingerprints, Ice pulled a nine-millimeter handgun out of his pocket and held it out with the butt end facing Raq. "Since you don't have a piece of your own, I asked Rashad if you could borrow his. End him."

Half Pint screamed behind his gag, his wide eyes pleading for mercy.

"Why me?" Raq asked, backing away from the gun.

"Because I need you to prove your loyalty to me. Show me you weren't planning to betray me too."

"Ice, I've had your back for eight years now," Raq said. "You should know by now I'd never turn on you."

"From now on, I'm Missouri. I'm not taking anyone's word for anything. You've got to show me. If I still have your loyalty, do what I ask you to do."

"You've got to pop your cherry sometime, right?" Dez asked. "Who better to practice on than a traitor?"

Raq's hands remained at her sides. "Before today, he wasn't a traitor. He was my friend."

"Ain't no room in this game for friendship."

Ice pressed the barrel of the gun to the back of Half Pint's head and pulled the trigger. Half Pint jerked and slumped sideways until both he and the chair he was duct taped to fell to the floor. Blood and brains spilled from what was left of his head. The acrid smell of piss and shit filled the room as Ice handed the smoking gun to Dez for disposal.

Ice stepped over the growing bloodstain on the floor and tapped his finger against Raq's heaving chest. "The next time I ask you to do something, your answer better be yes, not why, you hear me?"

Raq nodded mutely.

Bathsheba swallowed the rising bile in her throat when Ice turned his cold, unfeeling eyes on her.

"I wanted you to be here tonight so you could see how I deal with traitors." He buttoned his suit jacket as if he was wrapping up a business meeting instead of asking her and Raq to become accessories to murder. "Are you in or are you out?"

"I'm in," Bathsheba said quickly before he could question her loyalty as he had Raq's.

"Good. Now clean up this mess."

"Anything you say, boss," Raq said.

Bathsheba thought she heard a hint of challenge in Raq's voice. Perhaps her loyalty was up for grabs after all. If so, Bathsheba planned to be the one to claim it. If she didn't, she might soon find herself where Half Pint now was: bound to a chair, staring sightlessly at the ceiling while someone scraped her brains off the floor.

CHAPTER FIFTEEN

Raq jerked awake, her throat raw from screaming. Her next-door neighbor pounded on the wall between their apartments with what sounded like a broom handle.

"Keep it down in there, will you? Some of us have to go to work in the morning."

Raq smacked the wall with the side of her fist. "Shut up and go back to sleep."

"I will if you let me."

Embarrassed by losing control of the emotions she normally kept in check, Raq tossed the tangled covers aside and swung her legs over the side of the bed. As she held her head in her hands, she tried to stop the unwanted images from coursing through her mind. No matter what she did, she couldn't stop picturing Half Pint's head exploding after Ice fired a bullet into the back of his skull.

She wiped away the tears that came like clockwork every night. Half Pint was a pain in the ass who liked to play by his own rules, but he was just a kid. A seventeen-year-old kid who deserved to learn from his mistakes, not die from them. But die he had. And Raq watched him go. Then she had helped get rid of the evidence afterward.

Every time she closed her eyes, she saw Half Pint's body tense then go slack as the life drained out of him. She smelled the pungent stench of his bowels releasing. She saw herself cleaning up the mess Ice had made, scooping bits of brain and bone into a plastic bag after Bigfoot and Winky carted off Half Pint's body to a Dumpster in the Middle East. If Half Pint had been found somewhere else, the cops might be more motivated to solve the case rather than being so quick to pile it on top of the rest of the unsolved homicides committed by one or more unknown assailants. A number nearly higher than Raq could count.

Raq had never known Ice to do his own wet work before. Normally, he had someone else do it after he gave the order. That was how she knew the situation with Half Pint was about more than business for Ice. For some reason, it was personal.

Was Ice jealous of Half Pint's ambition or afraid the little runt might actually unseat him from his throne? Either way, he had proven his point. When it came to his money, his product, and his reputation, Ice wasn't to be played with.

In the days following Half Pint's disappearance, speculation ran rampant as to not only who was responsible but also who would take his place. Raq knew the answer to the first question but didn't have a clue about the answer to the second. She didn't care about answers to someone else's questions. What she wanted were answers to her own.

How had she not known what Half Pint was up to, and why was part of her glad he was gone? In a way, his death made her life easier. The other corner boys were easier to manage and none would risk taking the liberties Half Pint had. None of them would convince customers who couldn't pay in cash to barter their bodies instead. Not because they didn't want the sex but because they were too money-hungry to reach into their pockets to pay for it. Half Pint was the only one who had dared to do things his way because he thought he sold enough product to earn Ice's favor. Obviously, he had thought wrong.

Raq hadn't worked since Half Pint was killed. She had to get back out there before people started thinking she had developed a yellow streak. She wasn't scared. She just didn't have the stomach for the job like she used to.

She wasn't looking forward to hitting the streets again. Everyone would be nervous and edgy for a while, wondering if they were next on someone's hit list. Things would calm down in time. They always did. Yet Raq could find no comfort in the thought of returning to her old, familiar routine. It had been her job to keep Half Pint safe. To protect him from himself. She had failed at both. For that, she would never forgive herself.

She stared at her reflection in the rectangular mirror hanging over the sink. Silvery lines snaked through the discolored glass, giving her face a spooky appearance that fit perfectly with both her mood and the lateness of the hour. She looked as tired as she felt. She was tired of watching her friends die. Tired of running from the cops. Tired of fighting with rival crews. Tired of sleeping with one eye open.

She gripped the cracked sides of the porcelain sink to keep from putting her fist through the mirror.

"I don't want any more of this life," she said, feeling like crying again.

Working for Ice was like being in a gang. Once you were in, there was no getting out. She was stuck and she had nowhere to go. The realization was more crushing than a one-punch knockout.

She slowly sank to the floor, her boxers and tank top offering little protection from the cold tile. She wanted to feel safe. She wanted to be held by strong, loving arms. She wanted the little slice of heaven she had told Bathsheba about. She wanted it all and she wanted it now.

She reached for the phone that was never far from her side and called the woman who was never far from her heart.

"Hello?"

Bathsheba's voice was thick with sleep.

"I didn't know if it was too late to call or too early. Either way, I had to talk to you."

"What's wrong, Raq?"

Bathsheba's voice was clearer. Raq could tell she was wide-awake now. Awake and worried about her. She wasn't the only one. Raq felt more tears spring to her eyes. "I'm going crazy here and I need to see you. Can I come over?"

"Now?"

"I know it's late, but I need to talk to someone who understands. Someone who was there, you know what I mean?"

Raq didn't want to say too much over the phone, so she hoped she'd said enough to make Bathsheba understand where she was coming from.

"I know what you mean. I've been struggling, too."

Raq was glad to hear she wasn't the only one having a hard time dealing with things.

"Can I come see you?" she asked. "We don't have to do anything. I just—"

"It's okay, Raq," Bathsheba said softly. "We can do whatever you want." Then she said the words Raq hadn't been able to. "I need you, too."

Raq pulled herself to her feet, her heart relieved of a small share of its burden. "I'll be there as soon as I can."

"I'll be waiting."

Raq splashed cold water on her face to wash away the stink of the streets. Then she put on clothes—boots, hoodie, and oversized jeans—that allowed her to blend into them.

She walked with her head down and her shoulders bunched around her ears, hoping she looked unapproachable enough to keep the wolves at bay. She slowed when she neared the corner where Half Pint used to set up shop. In his place wasn't a member of Ice's crew but a member of King's.

Raq recognized the dealer right away, a lanky kid from East Biddle who thought he was LeBron James. He didn't have any of LeBron's basketball skills, but he must have owned every piece of LeBron-themed apparel Nike put out because Raq never saw him wearing anything without LeBron's name or face on it. His name was Gary, but for the last few years he had been calling himself The Heat. Raq often wondered if he'd change his name if LeBron bailed out on Miami at the end of his contract like he did Cleveland.

The Heat had enforcement on each end of the street, which meant Raq was outnumbered three to one. She started to cross the street to avoid trouble, but she couldn't let the matter drop. Ice and King had worked out a deal years ago, squashing the beef that had long existed between their rival crews. They had divided up the city and established a clear buffer zone between them. Ice's and King's dealers weren't supposed to come within two blocks of each other. King's people setting up shop on the edge of Ice's territory was one thing. Setting up inside it was another. One was a provocation that might spark another round of debates. This was an invitation to war.

When he saw Raq approach, The Heat signaled for his bodyguards to stay in their positions. Then he slowly lifted his oversized sweatshirt so Raq could see the butt of the gun sticking out of the waistband of his jeans.

Raq raised her hands to show she was unarmed. "I didn't come to squabble. I came to talk."

"About what?" The Heat asked, letting his sweatshirt drop.

"You're a bit outside of your territory, aren't you?"

He lifted his chin defiantly. "I go where I'm told and I was told to come here."

"This is Ice Taylor's territory."

"Things have changed since the last time you were out here. Word is your man Ice is slipping and my man King is taking advantage. You should learn to keep up."

"Are you sure you want to do this?"

When she took a step toward him, he reached for his gun to hold her at bay. "Like I said, I go where I'm told." She began to retreat as he pulled back the slide and chambered a round. She stopped moving when he raised the gun and pointed it at her face. "And from what I'm told, King wants to talk to you."

He put two fingers in his mouth and whistled sharply. Seconds later, headlights came on up the street and a dark gray SUV roared to life. The driver of the car did a U-turn and pulled up beside them. When the rear passenger's side door swung open, Raq saw three of King's men sitting inside, two in the front and one in the back.

"Get in," The Heat said, waving his gun toward the car. "King doesn't like to be kept waiting." His trigger finger twitched when Raq stood her ground. "I said, get in."

The words came out so slowly, each one felt like a separate sentence. Praying they wouldn't amount to a death sentence, Raq reluctantly climbed into the backseat of the car. "What kind of parlay takes place at three in the morning?" she asked as the driver roared away from the curb.

Seated beside her, King's man Breezy pulled his gun out of his jacket and placed it on his lap, the barrel pointing toward Raq's ribs. "The kind where our people talk and you listen."

Raq swallowed hard, trying not to show fear. King lived only a short distance away, but the trip felt like the longest ride of her life.

The car stopped in front of the project building where King continued to live despite the riches he had amassed. Unlike Ice, he didn't flaunt his money. He did, however, like to flex his muscle. Having his men snatch her off the street was his way of doing just that.

The two men in the front of the car stayed put while Breezy led Raq upstairs. Most of the tenants were on King's payroll so the building was like a veritable fortress. King's castle wasn't as fancy as Ice's, but it was even more secure. Fourteen floors of resistance lay between King and his enemies. And between Raq and freedom.

Bathsheba peeked between the blinds to get a better look at the deserted street. "She didn't show," she said into the phone pressed to her ear.

"What do you mean she didn't show?" Bill Carswell's voice had an edge to it. He sounded like a worried father sweating out his daughter's first date. Only the possible consequences of this encounter were much worse than the results of a few hours of teenage irresponsibility.

Bathsheba let the blinds fall back into place as she moved away from the window. "I mean I'm here and she's not."

"She's traveling on foot. Have you given her enough time to get to you?"

"She called me over two hours ago. Even if she was crawling on her hands and knees, she should have been here by now."

"Do you think she changed her mind?"

Bathsheba raised her free hand in frustration and let it fall. "I don't know what's going on."

"When you talked to her, how did she sound?"

Bathsheba chose her words carefully so she wouldn't betray her growing feelings for a woman who was one of the subjects of her investigation.

"Vulnerable, tired, and afraid." *Like she needed me to hold her and say everything was going to be okay.* "Like she needed a friend." *Like she needed me.*

"Do you think you can flip her?"

Bathsheba had been wondering the same thing ever since Raq had called.

"I think it's telling she turned to me in her time of need. Her faith in Ice is obviously shaken right now. But she's remained on his side for years despite previous ups and downs. Getting her to turn on him for good won't be easy, but I think I can do it. I just have to figure out a way to convince her to cut the cord. Did you find the evidence I told you about?"

After Half Pint's murder, Bathsheba and Raq had been ordered to clean up the mess. When they were done, they had dropped two trash bags in a Dumpster behind a nearby hospital.

"There was a ton of medical waste in the trash receptacle," Carswell said. "The tech guys are running DNA scans on what we found and cross-matching it against the samples we pulled from Jefferson's body to see if the new material can be positively identified as his. You don't think we'll get lucky enough to find Taylor's DNA in the bags you tossed, do you?"

"I doubt it. He was too careful to leave any DNA behind. And he was wearing gloves, so there's no gunshot residue on his hands. As for the clothes he was wearing during the shooting, they're in ashes somewhere. I heard him give the order to one of his underlings to throw them in the incinerator as soon as he returned to his apartment. Even if we managed to find the gun Dez Lassiter tossed, chances are Taylor's prints won't be on it and the serial number will be missing, making it impossible to trace. My eyewitness testimony might be enough to build a case around—with a murder charge, we could put Taylor away for life—but I want to make sure whatever charges we do file stick. With no physical evidence to tie Taylor to Jefferson's murder, he and his lawyer might find a way to wriggle out of our grasp just like they have too many times before."

"What about security cameras?"

"They're all over the lot, but I didn't see any inside the storage unit. If the ones outside the hospital are functioning properly, they might have captured Raq and me ditching the trash bags. To anyone watching the footage, we would look guiltier than Ice would. If we went to trial, it would be our word against his—and whoever he pays to provide him with an alibi."

"That's not enough to guarantee a verdict. I don't want this asshole getting off on a technicality or for lack of evidence."

"Neither do I. I want the case against Taylor to be airtight. We're almost there. I can feel it."

"I hope you're right," Carswell said with a heavy sigh.

"Wait," Bathsheba said, taking note of the air of defeat in his voice. "You're not considering pulling me, are you?"

Carswell sighed again. "I've got to be honest. I'm feeling some pressure from my superiors. They want results and they want them yesterday."

"I'm doing the best I can. Did they think I could waltz in here, bat my eyes a few times, and get Taylor to confess?"

"No, but I don't think they were planning on the op lasting more than a few weeks. You were undercover for almost a month before you made contact. Now you're coming up on two."

"Some ops take years."

"I know, but we don't have that luxury."

"That's not what I was told going into this. I was told we would have all the time we needed."

"I was there, remember? Look. I don't want to shut things down when we've invested so much time, money, and manpower in this thing, but if the talk I'm hearing downtown turns out to be true, I may not have a choice."

"Shit." Bathsheba sat down hard. Even though he wasn't in the same room, Carswell had just pulled the rug out from under her. "How long can you give me before you have to shut me down?"

He hesitated. "Two weeks. Maybe less."

"That's all?" Bathsheba asked incredulously.

"This is an election year, remember? Both the mayor and the governor are in the middle of tight races. They want Taylor in custody by election night."

"Because claiming responsibility could give them the votes they need to put them over the top."

"You know how the game is played."

"Funny. From where I'm sitting, it doesn't feel like a game. I'm putting my life on the line here and I'd appreciate a little backup."

"I've been here for you every step of the way. Like you, I do what I'm told. I don't make decisions. I only follow orders."

"I don't need lip service, sir. I need support."

"I hear you. I'll see what I can do."

When she ended the call, Bathsheba tried to resist the urge to panic. She had to remain calm. When the stakes were this high, she couldn't afford to make a mistake fueled by anger. Moreover, she couldn't afford to worry about things she couldn't control. Let Carswell worry about the logistics of the operation. She had to take care of the op itself.

She had returned to the Middle East to build a case against Ice Taylor and she wasn't leaving until she was done. If the department pulled its support, she would finish the job herself. She wasn't foolish enough to think she could do it on her own, however. She knew she needed help. And the woman whose help she needed the most was nowhere to be found.

❖

Raq's head was spinning. She felt like she was going in a million directions at once, and she had no idea which was the right way to turn.

King had asked her a question, and she had until Friday night to give him an answer. She should have told him to go fuck himself, but she hadn't wanted to piss him off when he had six armed guards flanking him. She had told him she'd think about his proposition just so he'd let her go, but the more she thought about it, the more it began to make sense. Times were changing. Maybe she needed to change along with them.

When King's men dropped her off on the corner, she called Bathsheba to see if it was safe to come over. After keeping her waiting for three hours, Raq didn't know what kind of welcome she could expect to receive, warm or cold. Bathsheba wasn't happy, but she said she could come over nevertheless.

"What happened to 'I'll be there as soon as I can'?" Bathsheba asked after she opened the door and invited her inside.

Relieved to be someplace safe for the first time in hours, Raq sank into the closest chair. "I was unavoidably detained."

"Is that why I haven't seen you at Ice's place the last couple of days?"

"You've been training there despite what happened?"

Bathsheba shrugged. "I had to keep up appearances."

Raq shook her head. Even though Bathsheba hadn't known Half Pint, had his death meant so little to her? "I can't pretend I didn't see Ice do what he did."

Bathsheba's voice grew gentle. "Is that what you wanted to talk to me about the first time you called? What Ice did? What he made us do?"

"Yeah."

"So talk to me."

Raq didn't know where to begin. The room felt too close. Too warm. She pulled off her hoodie so she could get some air. "Could I get something to drink first? I'll take a beer if you have one."

"It's six in the morning."

For the first time, Raq noticed Bathsheba was still in her pajamas. Her dark gray thermal Henley and plaid flannel pants made Raq feel overdressed.

"It's five o'clock somewhere, right?"

Bathsheba went to the kitchen and came back with a bottle of beer in one hand and a glass of orange juice in the other. Raq drained half of the beer before she set the bottle down.

"On the way over here," she said, wiping her mouth with the back of her hand, "I saw one of King's guys posted on Half Pint's corner."

"King's making a move on Ice's territory?"

"Seems like it."

"Have you told Ice yet?"

Uncertain whether she should answer the question, Raq drained the rest of her beer. "Not yet."

Bathsheba's eyes widened in shock. "Why not?"

"Because King offered me a job."

"Did you take it?" Bathsheba asked in a whisper.

Raq rolled the empty bottle between her palms, enjoying the feel of having something solid in her hands. "I told him I'd think about it. He wants an answer Friday night at the fights. If I take a dive against his girl, that means I've decided to throw in with him and his crew. If I fight her straight up, that means I've decided to stay with Ice."

"What if you throw the fight and he rescinds his offer? Then Ice would be out to get you and King wouldn't be around to protect you."

"That was the first thing I thought of."

Bathsheba curled her legs underneath her. "What was the second?"

"You. I thought about you and all the things we could do with the money King said he'd pay me. Then I thought about what Ice would do to you if I moved to King's outfit and left you behind. If Ice thought we were in on it together…."

Raq let her voice trail off because she didn't want to imagine how the sentence might end. Bathsheba was quiet for a long moment, no doubt filling in the blanks for herself.

"What does King want you to do?" she finally asked.

"All he wants me to do is box. I could leave all the other stuff behind. No more standing on corners. No more clean-up work."

"King's offering to pay you more money for less work? That doesn't make sense."

"That's what I said, too," Raq said with a hollow laugh. "He told me to consider part of it a signing bonus for switching teams. With the money he stands to make if I throw Friday night's fight, he'd have more than enough to pay me what he promised."

Bathsheba stared into the depths of her orange juice like the pulp floating in the glass was tea leaves she could use to tell the future. "With a deal like that, you'd be crazy to say no."

"If I betrayed a man like Ice, I'd be crazy to say yes."

"Even after what happened with Half Pint?"

"*Especially* after what happened with Half Pint." Sudden realization settled on her like a lead weight. "I can't leave."

"Why not?"

Raq carefully placed the empty beer bottle on the coffee table so she wouldn't be tempted to throw it against the wall and shatter it into a million pieces. "Because I don't have anywhere else to go."

"But King offered you a way out."

"He and Ice are about to go to war. Even if I switched sides, I'd still get caught in the middle." Unwanted tears stung her eyes. "I don't have anywhere to go, Bathsheba."

"But what if you did? If you had a way out—a *real* way out—would you take it?"

"That would depend on the price I had to pay. If the price was right, I'd pay it in a heartbeat. But I'm beginning to think that no matter how much I save, I'll never have enough."

She slumped in her chair. She couldn't remember the last time she had felt so dejected. Then Bathsheba stood and reached out to her.

"What are you doing?" Raq asked, staring at Bathsheba's outstretched hand.

Bathsheba smiled down at her. "Offering you a way out."

Raq's gut told her the solution Bathsheba was offering was only temporary at best, but she reached for the lifeline nevertheless. She felt uncharacteristically nervous as Bathsheba's fingers closed around hers, a probable byproduct of all the emotional upheaval she'd been through the past few days and especially tonight. But Bathsheba led her to the kitchen instead of the bedroom.

Bathsheba slid a chair away from the dining table and placed it in the middle of the room. "Have a seat." She must have seen the puzzled look on Raq's face because she immediately launched into an explanation. "When I was a kid," she said, setting a comb and a container of hair pomade on the counter, "I used to love Sundays. Every Sunday, my mother would sit me between her knees and do my hair so it would be fresh for school the next day."

As she talked, Bathsheba began the laborious process of loosening Raq's cornrows. Raq quickly became hypnotized by the sound of Bathsheba's voice and the rhythmic movement of her fingers.

"If the weather was warm," Bathsheba continued, "we'd sit on the front porch and watch the people in the neighborhood doing their thing. If it was cold like it is now, we'd sit in the kitchen with the oven door open to help heat up the room. We didn't have much when I was growing up, but it didn't matter. Because on Sundays we had love and that was enough."

The scene in Raq's house during her younger years had been eerily similar. She could picture the straightening comb resting on a red-hot stove burner, the metal teeth heating to the appropriate temperature so they could take out the knots a plastic comb couldn't tame. Except in her case, the comb had been used to straighten her attitude more often than her hair.

"When did it go wrong?" she asked, trying to forget the scars she had spent most of her life trying to hide. Both the ones that had been burned into her skin and the ones that had been etched into her soul.

"A very long time ago." Bathsheba's fingers paused for a few seconds, no doubt burdened by the weight of remembered pain. "I was ten when she started using. By the time I was thirteen, our roles were reversed. I was the mother and she was the child. Have you heard of that game Where's Waldo? My mornings began with a round of Where's Delilah? If she wasn't passed out somewhere in our apartment, I had to track her down, bring her home, get her cleaned up, and try to get some food into her before I put her in bed or let her sleep it off on the couch. Then I had to make breakfast for my sister and myself and get both of us ready for school."

"And now you're taking care of me." Raq closed her eyes as Bathsheba combed her hair.

Bathsheba chuckled softly as she used the comb to part Raq's hair. "It's not the same."

"No? How is it different?"

After she had divided Raq's hair into several sections, Bathsheba dipped her finger into the pomade and worked the gel into Raq's scalp. "If I wasn't around, you would still be able to take care of yourself. You're here because you want to be, not because you need to be."

Raq grabbed the chair and spun it to face Bathsheba. "I'm here because I want you." She took the comb out of Bathsheba's hands and placed it on the counter.

"I'm not done yet. I have to finish greasing your scalp, then I have to put your 'rows back in."

"Later. I want to tell you something first." She took Bathsheba's hands in hers. "When King's men snatched me up tonight, I wasn't afraid of what they might do to me. I've taken too many beatings in my time. Taking another wouldn't faze me. What scared me was the thought of losing you. Now that you're in my life, I can't imagine you not being a part of it. I had my doubts, but that's over now."

"Why did you doubt me?"

Bathsheba frowned and tried to back away. Raq, eager to relieve the hurt in Bathsheba's eyes before it began to fester and grow, held her fast. "I didn't doubt you. I didn't trust myself. I told myself you were trying to take my place. I realize now the only place you want to be is by my side. If you'll have me, I want to be at yours, too."

"If I'll have you? You've already got me." Bathsheba freed her hands so she could caress Raq's face. "You've had me from the day we met."

"You busted my chops that day. I put some of my best moves on you and you brushed all of them off." Raq smiled at the memory. "Why did you make me work so hard if we both wanted the same thing?"

"Some things are worth waiting for. Besides, I didn't want you to think I was a pushover."

"Baby, you are anything but that." Raq pulled Bathsheba into her lap. "What time do you have to be at work?"

"I don't." Bathsheba draped her arms over Raq's shoulders after she settled into a comfortable position. "Ice asked me to put in my notice after the New York trip so I quit the copy shop. Right now, my only job is keeping myself in shape."

Raq slipped her hands under Bathsheba's shirt and slid them over her increasingly well-defined abs. "From the feel of it, you're really good at your job."

The hitch in Bathsheba's breathing betrayed her growing excitement even before Raq saw the desire flaring in her eyes.

"There's always room for improvement." Bathsheba's voice shook as Raq's hands moved higher.

"Not from where I'm sitting. To me, you're perfect." Raq spread her fingers to cover more ground as she traveled up Bathsheba's sides and around to her back. "You're the best thing that's come into my life in years. I don't want to lose you."

Bathsheba ran her hands over Raq's hair, trying in vain to smooth the unruly curls the cornrows had left behind. "You won't."

"How do you know?"

Good question.

Raq seemed to have found what she had been looking for, but Bathsheba felt increasingly lost. She needed Raq on her side if she was to have any chance of putting Ice's organization out of business, but revealing her true identity to her didn't feel like the right move. Not now. It was still too soon, even though Carswell made it seem like it was almost too late. Raq had finally started to trust her. To care for her. She couldn't betray that trust by admitting she had been lying to her since day one. The bigger question was, how long had she been lying to herself?

She had tried to convince herself her attraction to Raq was tied to the false identity she had assumed when she went undercover. That it was something she could control. But her body's reaction to Raq's touch—the way her heart melted whenever Raq reached out to her—forced her to be honest. The person she was pretending to be wasn't the only one who wanted Raq. She did, too.

Bathsheba shuddered when Raq's fingers brushed against the underside of her breasts. She moaned when Raq gently pinched her nipples. She tightened her grip on Raq's shoulders and her hips began to move of their own volition, grinding in slow circles against Raq's firm belly.

Raq kissed her hard, parting her lips with her tongue and eagerly exploring her mouth. She slid her hands along Bathsheba's inner thighs, teasing the sensitive areas until Bathsheba felt like crying out for more. She was breathless when Raq finally broke the kiss. Breathless and almost painfully aroused. She couldn't remember when she had been touched like this. Tenderly. Firmly. Confidently. When she had felt like this. Wanted. Desired. And powerless to resist.

Her heart skipped a beat when Raq's hands moved to her hips because she knew what would come next.

When Raq posed the question she was surely about to ask, which part of Bathsheba would give the answer, the cop or the woman?

"We should move this to the bedroom, don't you think?" Raq asked, rising from the chair.

Bathsheba wrapped her legs around Raq's waist to keep from sliding to the floor. "Yes, we should."

Raq carried her to the bedroom as if she knew the way. Depending on how long she'd taken to search the apartment when Bathsheba was out of town, she might have the place memorized. Bathsheba forced those unpleasant thoughts from her mind as Raq laid her on the bed and covered her body with hers.

They pulled at each other's clothes, not stopping until their bodies had been laid as bare as their emotions.

Bathsheba sighed as Raq's weight settled on her again. Raq dressed like a boy on the streets, but she was all-girl underneath the tank top, boxers, and sagging jeans. Bathsheba ran her hands over the thick muscles in Raq's shoulders, arms, and back. Moving lower, she clutched Raq's churning hips, drawing them tighter against her and forcing them to slow their furious pace.

"Take it easy," she said, flipping Raq onto her back. "You don't have to rush. I want this to last. Don't you?"

Raq nodded. The slightly panicked look in her eyes let Bathsheba know she was unaccustomed to being in position to receive pleasure rather than provide it.

"Relax. I'm not going to hurt you." Bathsheba placed a hand over Raq's pounding heart. "You know I'd never do that, right?"

Raq nodded again.

"Then tell me what you want."

Bathsheba wanted her to voice her desires, not only so she could discover what Raq liked in bed, but so Raq could slowly begin to recover some of the power Ice had systematically taken from her over the years as he exercised control over nearly every facet of her life. The only places she was in control were in the ring and in bed. And sometimes not even there, depending on her opponent or her partner.

As she pondered the question, Raq looked like a kid who had been asked what she wanted for Christmas. She seemed torn between admitting what she really wanted and settling for what she could expect to receive.

"A massage," she said at last.

"Okay."

Bathsheba rubbed her hands together to warm them. She doubted Raq had ever been given the kind of massage she was about to provide. She wondered if she would be as responsive as she expected her to be.

Raq rolled onto her stomach and closed her eyes. She groaned in appreciation as Bathsheba firmly kneaded the muscles in her legs, back, and shoulders. Her body was dotted with scars. Bathsheba's curious fingers paused each time they encountered the physical reminder of an old wound, but she didn't question their origins. Instead, she kissed each one she encountered before eventually moving on.

Raq seemed self-conscious at first, then she began to blossom under the attention. As Bathsheba changed her firmness of the massage from hard to whisper-soft, she watched Raq open up even more.

Bathsheba trailed her fingertips over the curve of Raq's hips. Raq hissed in surprise and drew away from the contact.

Then she quickly came back for more, her hips rising to meet Bathsheba's waiting fingers.

Bathsheba slowly made her way up Raq's body. "Roll over," she said when she reached her shoulders again.

Raq dutifully rolled onto her back. Bathsheba didn't have to ask if she was ready for more. She could tell just by looking at her. Her nipples were hard and pearls of moisture glistened in the neatly trimmed hair at the apex between her legs.

"Damn, girl," she said as Bathsheba straddled her hips and gently kneaded her breasts. "You are good at this."

"Hold your praise. I'm just getting started."

"What else do you—"

Whatever Raq planned to say, she seemed to lose her train of thought as soon as Bathsheba's lips closed around her nipple. When her hips rose again, Bathsheba's hand was waiting to meet them. Bathsheba slipped her fingers between Raq's slick folds. Two fingers slid effortlessly inside.

Raq groaned deep in her throat. The veins on each side of her neck bulged as she thrust against Bathsheba's hand. Bathsheba met the pressure and returned it.

As she moved closer to the edge, Raq bit her lip to keep from crying out as if it was against some unwritten street code to show how much she was enjoying what was taking place between them. Bathsheba welcomed the challenge. Her goal immediately shifted from making Raq come to breaking through her defenses along the way.

"Trust me," she said in an urgent whisper. "Trust what you're feeling. Share it with me. Let me in."

Raq exhaled as if she had been waiting for the right moment to let down her guard. Her cry of pleasure began as a low moan and ended as a keening wail. Smooth muscles spasmed around Bathsheba's fingers, drawing them deeper. Bathsheba slowed her movements but didn't stop, drawing out Raq's orgasm until she couldn't tell when the first one ended and the second began.

"What are you trying to do, kill me?" Raq asked after she caught her breath.

"Not a chance." Bathsheba gently removed her fingers. "I haven't had my turn yet."

"Is there anything in particular you'd like me to do to you?" Raq asked with a sly smile as she traced lazy circles on Bathsheba's hip with the tip of one finger.

"Why don't you surprise me?"

"You know how much I love to eat," Raq said, licking her lips, "so why don't we take it from there?"

"I was hoping you'd say that."

Raq slowly made her way down Bathsheba's body, her kisses growing more reverent the lower she went. Bathsheba felt like a goddess being worshipped as Raq's mouth built a bridge between the sacred and the profane.

"God. Damn."

Bathsheba opened her legs wide enough for Raq to settle between them, then scisssored them around Raq's neck to hold her in place. Her body was on fire, baptized by a flame that burned so bright she closed her eyes to shield them from the glare.

"Yes," she said, tangling her fingers in Raq's unruly hair. "Right there."

Raq continued to stroke her with her tongue, alternating between slow and fast, soft and hard. Not knowing what to expect, Bathsheba lay back and allowed the sensations Raq produced to wash over her.

She forgot about the case and the time constraints she was under to bring it to a close. She forgot about Ice Taylor and the mind games he played with his employees. She forgot about the politicians who were making her life harder instead of easier. She forgot about everything except the one thing—the one person—who mattered most. Raq.

"Don't stop. Please don't stop."

The orgasm hit her like a sucker punch, slamming into her with a force she had never felt before. Thankfully, she didn't have far to fall. And Raq was there to catch her before she hit the canvas.

"Are you okay?" Raq asked.

When Raq kissed her, Bathsheba could taste her own juices on her tongue.

"Never better."

For one night at least, the words were true. She had no idea how long they would remain that way, but tonight she didn't care.

CHAPTER SIXTEEN

Raq woke with a pleasant heaviness in her limbs. She felt like she'd just gone twelve rounds with George Foreman before he gave up the sweet science to hawk religion and tabletop grills. Bright light streamed into the room and she squinted at the glare.

Wondering why nothing looked familiar, she took a moment to get her bearings. Then it hit her. She wasn't in her place. She wasn't in her bed. She was in Bathsheba's. Her clit twitched pleasurably as she remembered why she was waking up somewhere other than home. She reached for Bathsheba, but her side of the bed had grown cold.

"Good morning, sleepyhead. Or should I say good afternoon instead?"

Raq leaned over the side of the bed. Bathsheba was doing sit-ups on the floor. Based on the sheen of sweat coating her body, she had been at it for quite a while.

"What time is it?" Raq asked.

"Almost two," Bathsheba said, grunting with effort. "Do you want me to scrounge up something for lunch?"

"No, I have to head over to Ice's so I can tell him what's up. I'll grab something on the way. Do you have any clippers?"

"Somewhere. I'd have to find them. Why?"

Raq ran a hand over her hair, which felt like it was sticking up worse than Don King's. "I could use a trim before I go."

"How low?"

"All the way."

"You want me to shave it? Are you sure?" Bathsheba sat up and wrapped her arms around her knees. "You have a thick, beautiful head of hair and your cornrows are practically your trademark."

"I know, but it's time for a change. I've always wanted to go low, but I didn't have the guts to do it."

"But you do now?"

Raq grinned sheepishly. "You make me feel like I can do anything. People say I act like a man because of the way I dress and who I sleep with. If I shave my head, they'll probably say I want to turn into one, but the fact is I never feel more like a woman than when I'm with you."

"Thanks for the compliment, but I think you deserve more credit for that than I do. Come on. Let's get you hooked up."

Raq followed her to the kitchen just as she'd done the night before. Bathsheba rooted in drawers and cabinets as she tried to find a pair of electric clippers. Raq resisted the urge to give her hints because she wasn't supposed to know where they were.

"Bingo," Bathsheba said at last.

"Sweet."

Bathsheba plugged the clippers into the wall and wrapped a towel around Raq's shoulders to catch the falling hairs. "Last chance to change your mind."

"I'm sure. Let's do it."

"Okay." Bathsheba flipped the power switch with her thumb and the clippers buzzed to life. "Here goes nothing."

Bathsheba adjusted the blade length and pressed the guard against the side of Raq's head. Raq expected the clippers to snatch and grab her hair, but she didn't feel any discomfort as Bathsheba moved in slow, even strokes. When she was done and she handed Raq a mirror so she could inspect the results, Raq felt liberated. She felt complete. She felt truly herself for the first time in her life.

"How do I look?" she asked, seeking Bathsheba's approval.

"You look…powerful."

That was exactly how she felt.

"Thanks," she said, giving Bathsheba a quick kiss. "I'm going to take a shower and hit the road. I'll meet up with you later, okay?"

"You'd better. I'd hate to think last night was a one-time thing."

"Only if you want it to be." Raq hadn't considered the possibility Bathsheba might not be as serious about their relationship as she was. The thought left her suddenly terrified.

"I don't."

"Good. Because neither do I. Keep doing what you were doing, workout queen. I'll call you later."

Bathsheba smiled as Raq gave her a playful smack on the butt on her way out of the room. Raq showered and changed into the clothes she had been wearing the night before. She gave Bathsheba a lingering kiss at the door before leaving to meet up with Ice. She had been gone only a few minutes when Bathsheba's doorbell rang.

"What did you forget?" Bathsheba asked, opening the door without bothering to look through the peephole to see who was standing on the other side.

Dez looked her up and down, his mirrored sunglasses reflecting her own image back at her. "Nothing, Ma," he said with an appreciative suck of his teeth, "but you make me wish I had. Is Raq here?"

"No, she left a few minutes ago. She's headed to Ice's to let him know King is making a move on his territory."

"We already know all about it. That's why Ice sent me to rally the troops. Get dressed. You're coming with me."

"Give me five minutes. I'll be right out."

She tried to close the door, but Dez blocked it with his hand.

"That's okay. I can wait." He slipped his sunglasses into his jacket pocket as he stepped into the apartment. "You do what you got to do. I'll be right here when you're done."

Bathsheba grabbed some clothes from the bedroom. She locked the bathroom door behind her, but she knew the flimsy thing wouldn't protect her if Dez wanted to get at her.

She showered and dressed in almost record time. Dez hadn't displayed a sense of urgency, but she felt one nevertheless. She tried to call Carswell while she allowed the water to run, but the call went to voicemail. He was supposed to be available to her around the clock. She wondered if the cutbacks he had hinted at during their last conversation included his man hours as well. If so, she was in deep shit. She had no choice but to leave him a message.

"I'm on the move," she said as quietly as she could. "I'll be traveling in a black Navigator with custom plates DEZSNAV. Let me spell it out for you. That's Delta Epsilon Zulu Sierra

November Alpha Victor. If you have any unmarked units in the area, mobilize them now. I need a tail. A street war's about to go down and we need to get a handle on it before it gets out of control."

She ended the call and quickly began another. Pop Walker had offered to help with her investigation. There wasn't much he could do at his advanced age, but she made it a point to let him know her whereabouts at all times. If she went missing, she wanted someone to notice the loss.

"What's going on, baby girl?" he asked.

"I'm meeting up with Ice and I wanted you to know."

"Are you going to his apartment or the restaurant?"

"I don't know. It could be either one."

"Okay. Call me when you're done."

"I will. If you don't hear from me by nine tonight, you know what to do."

"You can count on me."

She ended the call, turned off the water, and waited a few minutes before she opened the door.

"You ready?" Dez rose from his seat when she stepped out of the bathroom.

Bathsheba took an involuntary look at the ceiling to see if all the tiles were in place. She'd gotten rid of the computer after Raq searched the apartment, but she hadn't managed to purge herself of the paranoia that went with it. "Yeah, I'm ready."

Dez tossed the magazine he had been reading on the coffee table and slipped his sunglasses back on. "Then let's roll."

On the street, he climbed into the front of the Navigator and she sat next to Bigfoot in the back.

"Buckle up," Dez said as Rico turned the key in the ignition. "We wouldn't want anything to happen to you, would we?"

Bathsheba pulled the seat belt across her body and snapped the restraint into place. "What's the matter? Don't you trust Rico's skills behind the wheel?"

She meant the comment as a joke, but Dez, Rico, and Bigfoot didn't laugh, the boys bonding against the lone girl in their midst. "Accidents happen," Dez said flatly.

Bathsheba flinched when the door locks engaged. Thanks to the child safety locks on the rear doors, she was effectively trapped.

"How many people are coming to this meeting?" she asked.

Dez shrugged. "I'm not the one in charge of invitations. I'll find out when you do."

"Is it being held at Ice's place?"

"Nah. He doesn't do business out of his home if he can help it. A man's home is his castle, right?"

"We can't be going to Miss Marie's. We already passed it."

"There are too many eyes and ears at Miss Marie's. We don't want anyone who doesn't need to know to find out what's going on. The situation is too volatile. When we move on King, we need to take him by surprise. Otherwise, he'll barricade himself inside his apartment building and we'll never be able to get to him."

"So where are we meeting, some safe house the cops don't know about?"

Dez and Rico exchanged a look, the universal expression of men who are tired of answering a woman's questions.

"Keep your shorts on. We'll be there soon enough. You're not nervous, are you?"

"This is my first sit-down. I don't know what to expect. I feel unprepared."

"I saw how you handled yourself in New York. You'll be fine."

Bathsheba didn't feel comforted by the vote of confidence. Dez's demeanor seemed a bit off to her. Rico's and Bigfoot's, too. They seemed like they were going out of their way to play it cool, which made it seem like they had something to hide.

She pulled out her cell phone. The burner didn't have a GPS, which made it impossible to trace, but she liked having it close at hand. Something tangible she could hold onto.

"Who are you calling?" Dez asked.

She had intended to text Carswell the address of the intersection they had just passed through because she hadn't noticed anyone on their tail, but she decided it was too risky. Lately, Ice had started insisting she check her cell phone at the door. If someone scrolled through her messages, the one to Carswell might raise a red flag.

"I'm texting Raq. I need to tell her something before I see her face-to-face."

"Put the phone down," Dez said after he and Rico exchanged another look.

Bathsheba continued typing her message. "In a minute. I'm almost done."

Dez turned in his seat. "Did I stutter? When I say put the phone down, I mean now, not five minutes from now."

"Fine. I'll turn it off." Bathsheba hit Send before her thumb pressed the Power button.

Had fun the other night, she had typed, *but I think we have even bigger things in store today.*

She held up the phone to show Dez the darkened display.

"It's off, okay?"

"Good. Now give it here."

"Why?"

"You don't want to take a chance on it going off during the meeting, do you? Don't worry. You'll get it back afterward."

"I'll make sure it's on silent."

"Not good enough. We're about to go to war. We need to stay focused. Our people don't have time to be beefing with their baby mamas or having phone sex with their girlfriends. That includes you."

Dez held out his hand and beckoned for the phone. After Bathsheba handed it over, Dez tossed it in the glove compartment and slammed the door shut. She noticed he didn't reach for his own phone or ask Rico and Bigfoot to give up theirs.

Bathsheba's unease gave way to a darker emotion. She felt fear—real fear—for the first time since she had climbed into the car.

"What's really going on?"

Dez pulled off his sunglasses so she could see his eyes.

"I don't know, cop. Why don't you tell me?"

CHAPTER SEVENTEEN

Raq was halfway to Ice's apartment when she received a text asking her to meet him at the storage unit. She was hoping she wouldn't have to set foot in that place for a while. Now she was heading there for the second time in less than a week.

She pulled the string above her head to let the bus driver know she wanted to get off. She caught another bus heading the opposite direction of her original destination and disembarked a few blocks from the storage unit. She hoofed it the rest of the way.

She expected the lot to be teeming with activity since it was still relatively early in the day, but the place was practically deserted. The only cars in the lot belonged to Ice, Dez, and several members of Ice's crew.

In his text, Ice had said they needed to talk about the moves King was making. If she had known he planned to invite so many people to hear what she had to say, she would have taken time to prepare.

She used the walk across the lot to organize her thoughts. To get the nightmarish images of Half Pint's murder out of her head so she could concentrate on business. She went over everything King and The Heat had said so she would be sure not to leave anything out. She wanted Ice to have all the ammunition he needed to come out on top. In the coming turf war between Ice and King, she planned to be on Ice's side. He had his issues—and she had her issues with him—but better the devil you knew than the one you didn't.

She didn't know how much longer she planned on doing what she did for a living, but with Bathsheba's help, she wouldn't have to keep doing it forever. Together, they could find a way out. A place just for them. She had been on her own for nearly half her life. She had drifted from one temporary family to another. Now she had the chance to build something permanent. Something real. And to think she had almost thrown it away.

She had never met a woman she trusted enough to give her heart to. Then she met Bathsheba. She'd had her doubts about her, too, but those doubts were gone now. She couldn't wait to get this meeting over with so she and Bathsheba could get back to what they had been doing all morning. What Raq hoped they'd be doing for years to come.

She hadn't realized having someone to go home to could feel this good. Just thinking about Bathsheba put a smile on her face. As she walked through the lot, she was cheesing harder than a kid who'd just had her braces removed after spending five years with metal mouth.

"Whatever you're on, I want some," Hercules said when he saw her coming.

"Nah, man. I don't feel like sharing." She gave him a pound. "Am I the last one?"

"Yeah. Everyone else is waiting for you inside."

"Let's get to it then."

Hercules opened the door and they ducked underneath. He let the door fall when they were safely on the other side.

The unit was big, but it was almost too small to hold all the people crammed into it. Folks were packed so tight Raq had a good idea how sardines felt on their way out of the factory.

Everyone was standing in a circle like they were the Knights of the Round Table. Ice, of course, was King Arthur. The circle broke when Raq and Hercules entered the room. All the talking stopped and everyone turned to look at them.

"The guest of honor has finally arrived," Ice said from the top of what was left of the circle.

He beckoned her forward, but Raq hung back, trying to figure out why the situation didn't feel right. Then Ice stepped aside and she saw Bathsheba on her knees with her hands tied behind her back and a gag in her mouth.

Raq's first instinct was to run to her, but her feet wouldn't move. Hercules helped her out with a hard shove to the small of her back. She stumbled and nearly went down as the circle closed around her.

Bathsheba looked up at her, her eyes pleading for help, mercy, or both.

"What's this about?" Raq asked as the sea of angry faces drew closer. "I thought we were here to talk about King. I thought Bathsheba was your girl."

"King can wait. And I thought *you* were *my* girl." Ice put his arm around her neck, his grip so tight she could barely breathe. "I trusted you, Raq. I brought you into my organization and treated you like family. This is how you repay me, by bringing an undercover cop into our ranks?"

"A what?"

Nothing Ice was saying made sense. The words wouldn't register. Bathsheba was a cop? Raq's instincts about her had been right all along?

"She's a what?"

Ice drew back in genuine surprise. He examined her face to see if she was lying. "You didn't know." He laughed bitterly. "Seems like I'm not the only one she lied to."

He snapped his fingers and Dez slipped a small cloth pouch into his hand. The pouch reminded Raq of the Crown Royal bag her mother used to use as a makeshift piggy bank back in the day, but she had a feeling this bag didn't contain anything she wanted to beg, borrow, or steal.

"I have a way for you to make it better. For you and for her," Ice said, loosening the pouch's strings. "Don't give me that innocent look. You're lucky your ass isn't on the floor with her. When were you going to tell me about your little meeting with King? When you showed up to give me your two weeks' notice?"

She didn't ask him how he knew about King's job offer because she knew what his answer would be: he knew everything. She didn't know why she had thought she could keep something from him. It had been foolish to even try. Now she was about to pay the price. Her and Bathsheba both.

"This is my world, Raq. No one comes in or out of it unless I say so." He pulled a gun out of the bag and handed it to her, butt-end first. "I want this bitch dealt with and I want you to do it for me."

Raq didn't take the gun.

"No."

"Excuse me?" Ice held a finger to his ear. "I don't hear so well on this side. What did you say?"

Raq squared her shoulders. "I said no."

Ice scowled. "Do you remember what I said the last time I asked you to take care of someone for me and you refused? The only correct response to the request I just made is 'Yes, boss.'"

Dez, Winky, and Bigfoot drew their guns.

"Do her or my boys do you."

"I'm not going to shoot her," Raq said, desperately trying to find a way out of this mess that would allow her to live with herself in the morning. If, that was, she was still breathing by then. She didn't know who to believe, Bathsheba or Ice. She needed to hear Bathsheba's side of the story—to get her version of the truth—but, thanks to the gag in her mouth, Bathsheba wasn't talking. So Raq did the only thing she could do. She stalled for time until she could figure out her next move. "Shooting her would end things too quickly. Don't you want her to suffer first?"

"You bet your ass, I do."

Raq clenched and unclenched her fists to hide the fact that her hands were shaking. This was her crew. They were her people. Her fam. She had sweated with them. She had bled with them. They were supposed to have her back. They were supposed to make her feel safe. But she couldn't remember the last time she had felt so scared.

"I can give you what you want."

Ice looked intrigued. "What do you have in mind?"

"Let's settle this where I settle everything else: in the ring."

"Fine," Ice said, "but let me make something clear right now. Two of you are going into the ring, but only one of you is coming out of it. For your sake, you'd better hope it's you."

"Don't worry. It will be."

For years, boxing had been Raq's salvation. Today, it would either cost her her life or save it once and for all.

CHAPTER EIGHTEEN

Bathsheba had always wondered if she could beat Raq in a fair fight, but this match-up was anything but fair. The "ring" didn't consist of a canvas-covered platform surrounded by parallel lines of rope but a cadre of snarling, angry men who thought they were part of the action. Every time she drifted too close to them, she caught a blow from behind.

She had taken so many kidney punches she was going to be pissing blood for a week. If, that was, she somehow made it out of the room alive. Even if she managed to defeat Raq, she knew there was no way Ice would let her live.

This was it.

But she couldn't curl into in a ball and give up. She had to keep fighting. Keep thinking there was a chance—slim as it might be—she could find a way out.

Raq was unquestionably stronger, but Bathsheba was quicker and had more endurance. If she could keep avoiding Raq's punches, perhaps she could buy enough time to land one of her own. If she timed it just right, one would be all she needed.

Employing the defensive skills Zeke had taught her, she used constant movement to make herself an elusive target. Bobbing, weaving, and circling from one side of the ring to the other. The crowd booed at the lack of action, but she wasn't trying to earn brownie points from them or actual ones from the nonexistent judges. She was trying to stay alive.

"Fight me, you coward," Raq said through clenched teeth.

Bathsheba could sense Raq's growing frustration as she continued to stalk an opponent who refused to be caught. Just the breeze from one of Raq's many swings and misses was almost enough to knock her out. She didn't want to feel the kind of damage the punches could inflict if they actually connected.

"We don't have to do this," she said, warding off more cheap shots from the interfering crowd.

She kicked out blindly behind her. The stacked heel of her boot connected with someone's shin. Her attacker yelped in pain. She'd aim higher next time. A shot to the balls might be enough to get the bloodthirsty horde to back off. No, she knew that was wishful thinking. The men in this room wouldn't be satisfied until Raq served up her head on a silver platter.

She had never pictured herself as John the Baptist or Raq as Salome, but there they were filling the roles.

"You lied to me."

Raq rushed at her, but Bathsheba managed to pin her arms at her sides and get her in a clinch.

"Not about everything," she whispered as Raq furiously tried to break the hold she had on her. "Not about the way I feel for you."

"Did you really mean all those things you said or was it all a part of your cover?"

Raq jerked free and dug a right hand into Bathsheba's ribs that made her knees buckle. Bathsheba pushed Raq away to put some distance between them.

She couldn't reconcile herself to the fact that the hands that had brought her so much pleasure a few hours before were now trying to cause her nearly as much pain. She wasn't surprised. Just disappointed they had gone from such an incredible high to such a crushing low so quickly.

Why, exactly? Because she had underestimated her opponent.

After Dez had dragged her out of his car at gunpoint and forced her into the storage unit, Ice had let her know he hadn't taken her actions in New York as definitive proof she could be trusted. He had directed his people to keep digging into her cover story until one of them—a computer geek living in the basement of his parents' house—found a photo of her online. A photo of her in uniform.

Ice had thrown the photo in her face as proof of his superiority over her. Then he had waved it in Raq's face like a red flag in front of an enraged bull. The damned article Bathsheba had thought no one in Ice's crew would ever see had turned out to be her undoing.

"Sometimes," Ice had said as he placed a filthy gag in her mouth, "the bad guys win."

They were certainly winning now.

Bathsheba defended herself from Raq's onslaught as best she could, but she didn't throw any punches of her own. She simply couldn't bring herself to lash out at the woman she loved. Raq, however, didn't share her dilemma. Because Raq's love had apparently turned to hate.

When Raq feinted to her right, Bathsheba instinctively moved in the opposite direction and ran straight into a left hook to her midsection that doubled her over.

"Oh, that one hurt," someone in the crowd yelled as the onlookers screamed for more.

Throwing a heavy barrage of punches, Raq moved in for the kill while Bathsheba tried to keep her at bay long enough to catch her breath and recover from the blow. She held her hands in front of her face and moved her body left and right, absorbing the brunt of the assault with her shoulders and forearms.

"You got her in trouble now, Raq," someone else said. "Take her head off."

Bathsheba peeked through her defenses. What she saw surprised her. Raq's eyes were filled not with malice but regret. Bathsheba tried to reach her before Raq allowed her own defensive shields to slide back into place.

"I love you, Raq. Do you think I would lie about that? We can get through this, but you have to trust me. Do you trust me?"

Raq dropped her hands, giving Bathsheba the opening she needed. She quickly tapped her fists and drew back to throw a right, but Raq sidestepped and threw a right cross Bathsheba couldn't avoid, even though she saw it coming. The punch landed flush on her jaw. She saw an explosion of light, then nothing as she crumpled unconscious to the floor.

"Trust is for suckers."

Raq raised her arms in triumph as she stood over the body of yet another vanquished opponent. She felt no pleasure in this victory, however. Only remorse for what could have been. For what she was about to do. Her life was composed of a series of tough choices. And now she was faced with the toughest choice of all. A choice that was becoming harder and harder to make. The choice between loyalty and love.

Ice nudged Bathsheba's leg with the toe of his polished wingtip to make sure she was really down for the count.

"Damn, girl. You nearly knocked her into next week."

Finally realizing where her true loyalties lay, Raq steeled herself for the challenge looming before her. "That's what you pay me for, isn't it?"

Ice raised an eyebrow. "I thought King was your boss now."

"You're my dog. You know that. Now give me that piece so I can end this in style."

Ice's eyebrow crept even closer to his hairline as he handed her the gun she had repeatedly refused to take.

The gun felt heavier than Raq had expected it to. How could something so small carry so much weight? She racked the slide the way she had seen so many of her friends and enemies do in the past.

"She really put a hurting on you, huh?" Ice asked.

"Not half as bad as the one I'm going to put on you."

She put her finger on the trigger and pointed the gun in Ice's direction. His eyes bulged as he took a halting step backward, his hands raised in surrender.

"Do you honestly think you can shoot your way past every motherfucker in here?"

Dez, Bigfoot, and Winky already had their guns drawn. The rest were reaching for theirs.

"I'm not planning on shooting them. Just you. And even if they tag me, I'm taking you with me before I go."

Ice's eyes grew wild with fear. He was finally getting a taste of what he had put countless other people through over the years. She didn't plan to stop until he was full.

"Drop your toolies. Now, goddammit!" Ice frantically waved for Dez and the others to lower their guns. Amid much grumbling, they complied with his request.

Raq kept a close eye on Ice as she knelt next to Bathsheba's limp body. She gripped Bathsheba's shoulder with her free hand and gave her a rough shake. Bathsheba moaned but didn't open her eyes.

"Wake up. I didn't hit you that hard." She gave Bathsheba another shake. "Come on, B. I need you. I can't do this by myself."

Bathsheba's eyes slowly fluttered open. She looked around in confusion, then scrambled to her feet.

"Are you carrying?" Raq asked.

Bathsheba nodded, then grimaced as if the movement hurt. Raq's heart sank. A dark purple bruise had already started to form along the line of Bathsheba's jaw. She must have hit her harder than she thought.

Bathsheba reached for the .38 strapped to her ankle.

"A throwdown," Raq said. "Bigfoot always misses those when he does a pat down."

"I noticed," Bathsheba said, training her gun at Ice's head. She gave Raq an appreciative look out of the corner of her eyes. "Since you're running this show, what's the plan?"

"Ice is going to give us an escort out of here." Raq grabbed him by his collar and pointed him toward the door. "Nice and slow," she said as she held the gun against his back.

He offered some token resistance but quickly quieted down when she pressed the barrel of the gun into his kidney.

"Even if I walk you out of here, you'll both be dead before night falls. I may even pull the trigger myself."

Bathsheba walked behind them, covering their rear. "That's going to be hard for you to do from behind bars. I plan on putting you there personally."

He laughed bitterly. "You and what army?"

Raq motioned for Hercules to lift the storage unit door. More squad cars than she had ever seen in her life had the place surrounded.

Bathsheba forced Ice to his knees. "Me and this army."

As uniformed officers swarmed into the storage unit, a gray-haired man in a rumpled suit and a spaghetti sauce-stained tie waddled over to Bathsheba.

"You got him."

"Carswell, I never thought I'd be so happy to see you," Bathsheba said. "You understood my text?"

"It took a while for your CI and me to figure it out. We're older and slower than we used to be, but we get there eventually."

"Better late than never."

"What text?" Raq asked. She wondered if they were talking in police code because they sounded like they were speaking a secret language.

Bathsheba cut her eyes at Ice. Raq guessed she didn't want to reveal the name of her confidential informant in front of him. Good thing. Ice treated potential witnesses like he did toilet paper. Both were equally disposable. "Let's just say you aren't the only person who had my back today. When did you decide you could trust me?"

Raq shrugged, unsure how to put what she was feeling into words. Ice had been in her life for the past eight years, but

Bathsheba *was* her life. "I've been trusting you since the day we met. You haven't let me down yet."

"I don't intend to start."

Carswell cleared his throat to get their attention. Then he handed Bathsheba a pair of handcuffs. "I'll let you do the honors."

"With pleasure."

Bathsheba cuffed Ice's wrists and began to recite the charges against him. "Isaac Taylor, you are under arrest for drug trafficking, the kidnapping of a peace officer, and the murder of Rashad Jefferson."

"You're trying to saddle me with a murder rap?" Ice asked after Bathsheba read him his rights. "Really? My lawyer will have me out of jail within forty-eight hours and I will have each one of your asses in seventy-two. Where's your evidence? Where are the witnesses lining up to testify against me?"

Raq stood in front of him. "The line starts right here." She hoped once it started, it wouldn't stop until it snaked out the courthouse door. It was time—finally time—for Ice's reign of terror to come to an end. And she would help make it happen.

Ice was momentarily speechless. He looked defeated. He looked like he thought she'd never turn against him. Until a few minutes ago, she never thought she would either. But her love for Bathsheba had proved to be more powerful than her loyalty to Ice.

She wished Bathsheba had told her she was a cop— hearing it from Ice had momentarily made her wonder if Bathsheba had simply been using her to get to him—but, in her heart, she knew Bathsheba's feelings for her were real, and she understood why Bathsheba had kept the fact that she was five-oh to herself. While she tried to bring Ice down,

Bathsheba needed to protect not only herself but Raq as well. Now it was Raq's turn to protect her. And if Raq had her way, from now on, there would be no more secrets between them. No matter what the cost.

Trying to save face as his kingdom crumbled all around him, Ice acted tough for the sake of the men being herded past him into the waiting police vans.

"You won't live to see the trial."

"Come and get me," Raq said. "I'll be waiting."

"He's right, you know," Bathsheba said after she deposited Ice in the back of a squad car. "If you stay in the Middle East, someone's going to be gunning for you every day until the case goes before a judge. We have to put you in a safe house until the trial starts."

"I'm not running."

"And I'm not taking a chance on losing you." Bathsheba laid a hand on her arm. "We're family now. I protect what's mine."

Family. Something Raq thought she'd never have had become something she would fight not to lose. This time, she had someone in her corner who would fight just as hard for her.

"We'll talk about it later, okay?" she said. "What time are you going to be home?"

"Not for a while. It's going to take hours to process and book everyone. When I'm done, I can't go back to the neighborhood, either. People are going to be gunning for me, too. Until Ice is behind bars for good, neither one of us is safe."

Raq smiled. "We talked about running away together. Looks like we get our chance."

Bathsheba smiled back. "We'd be on the run, but at least we'd be together. Is that what you want?"

"I want to be with you. Today. Tomorrow. Forever, if you let me."

"I want that, too."

Even though Raq wanted nothing more than to remain in this moment with Bathsheba and relive it over and over, her thoughts quickly turned to unfinished business. "What about King? He was already making moves on Ice's territory before this happened. Now you know he's going to try to take over completely."

"When the opportunity presents itself, we'll get him, too."

Raq couldn't hide her surprise. "*We*? You want to team up again?"

"Now that you and I are on the same side, you don't expect me to catch every kingpin in Baltimore without you, do you?"

"Nah, baby." Raq drew her into her arms. "I'll always have your back."

Just as she knew Bathsheba would always have hers.

About the Author

Mason Dixon lives, works, and plays somewhere in the South. She and her partner enjoy grilling, traveling, and fighting for control of the remote. *Charm City* is her second novel. Her previous work is Lambda Literary Award finalist *Date With Destiny*. As Yolanda Wallace, she has published six novels—*In Medias Res*, *Rum Spring*, *Lucky Loser*, Lammy Award-winner *Month of Sundays*, *Murphy's Law*, and *The War Within*. Mason can be reached at authormasondixon@gmail.com.

Books Available from Bold Strokes Books

Let the Lover Be by Sheree Greer. Kiana Lewis, a functional alcoholic on the verge of destruction, finally faces the demons of her past while finding love and earning redemption in New Orleans. (978-1-62639-077-5)

Blindsided by Karis Walsh. Blindsided by love, guide dog trainer Lenae McIntyre and media personality Cara Bradley learn to trust what they see with their hearts. (978-1-62639-078-2)

About Face by VK Powell. Forensic artist Macy Sheridan and Detective Leigh Monroe work on a case that has troubled them both for years, but they're hampered by the past and their unlikely yet undeniable attraction. (978-1-62639-079-9)

Blackstone by Shea Godfrey. For Darry and Jessa, their chance at a life of freedom is stolen by the arrival of war and an ancient prophecy that just might destroy their love. (978-1-62639-080-5)

Out of This World by Maggie Morton. Iris decided to cross an ocean to get over her ex. But instead, she ends up traveling much farther, all the way to another world. Once there, only a mysterious, sexy, and magical woman can help her return home. (978-1-62639-083-6)

Kiss The Girl by Melissa Brayden. Sleeping with the enemy has never been so complicated. Brooklyn Campbell and

Jessica Lennox face off in love and advertising in fast-paced New York City. (978-1-62639-071-3)

Taking Fire: A First Responders Novel by Radclyffe. Hunted by extremists and under siege by nature's most virulent weapons, Navy medic Max de Milles and Red Cross worker Rachel Winslow join forces to survive and discover something far more lasting. (978-1-62639-072-0)

First Tango in Paris by Shelley Thrasher. When French law student Eva Laroche meets American call girl Brigitte Green in 1970s Paris, they have no idea how their pasts and futures will intersect. (978-1-62639-073-7)

The War Within by Yolanda Wallace. Army nurse Meredith Moser went to Vietnam in 1967 looking to help those in need; she didn't expect to meet the love of her life along the way. (978-1-62639-074-4)

Escapades by MJ Williamz. Two women, afraid to love again, must overcome their fears to find the happiness that awaits them. (978-1-62639-182-6)

Desire at Dawn by Fiona Zedde. For Kylie, love had always come armed with sharp teeth and claws. But with the human, Olivia, she bares her vampire heart for the very first time, sharing passion, lust, and a tenderness she'd never dared dream of before. (978-1-62639-064-5)

Visions by Larkin Rose. Sometimes the mysteries of love reveal themselves when you least expect it. Other times they hide behind a black satin mask. Can Paige unveil her masked stranger this time? (978-1-62639-065-2)

All In by Nell Stark. Internet poker champion Annie Navarro loses everything when the Feds shut down online gambling, and she turns to experienced casino host Vesper Blake for advice—but can Nova convince Vesper to take a gamble on romance? (978-1-62639-066-9)

Vermilion Justice by Sheri Lewis Wohl. What's a vampire to do when Dracula is no longer just a character in a novel? (978-1-62639-067-6)

Switchblade by Carsen Taite. Lines were meant to be crossed. Third in the Luca Bennett Bounty Hunter Series. (978-1-62639-058-4)

Nightingale by Andrea Bramhall. Culture, faith, and duty conspire to tear two young lovers apart, yet fate seems to have different plans for them both. (978-1-62639-059-1)

No Boundaries by Donna K. Ford. A chance meeting and a nightmare from the past threaten more than Andi Massey's solitude as she and Gwen Palmer struggle to understand the complexity of love without boundaries. (978-1-62639-060-7)

Timeless by Rachel Spangler. When Stevie Geller returns to her hometown, will she do things differently the second time around or will she be in such a hurry to leave her past that she misses out on a better future? (978-1-62639-050-8)

Second to None by L.T. Marie. Can a physical therapist and a custom motorcycle designer conquer their pasts and build a future with one another? (978-1-62639-051-5)

Seneca Falls by Jesse Thoma. Together, two women discover love truly can conquer all evil. (978-1-62639-052-2)

A Kingdom Lost by Barbara Ann Wright. Without knowing each other's fates, Princess Katya and her consort Starbride seek to reclaim their kingdom from the magic-wielding madman who seized the throne and is murdering their people. (978-1-62639-053-9)

Season of the Wolf by Robin Summers. Two women running from their pasts are thrust together by an unimaginable evil. Can they overcome the horrors that haunt them in time to save each other? (978-1-62639-043-0)

The Heat of Angels by Lisa Girolami. Fires burn in more than one place in Los Angeles. (978-1-62639-042-3)

Desperate Measures by P. J. Trebelhorn. Homicide detective Kay Griffith and contractor Brenda Jansen meet amidst turmoil neither of them is aware of until murder suspect Tommy Rayne makes his move to exact revenge on Kay. (978-1-62639-044-7)

The Magic Hunt by L.L. Raand. With her Pack being hunted by human extremists and beset by enemies masquerading as friends, can Sylvan protect them and her mate, or will she succumb to the feral rage that threatens to turn her rogue, destroying them all? A Midnight Hunters novel. (978-1-62639-045-4)

Wingspan by Karis Walsh. Wildlife biologist Bailey Chase is content to live at the wild bird sanctuary she has created on Washington's Olympic Peninsula until she is lured beyond the safety of isolation by architect Kendall Pearson. (978-1-60282-983-1)

Windigo Thrall by Cate Culpepper. Six women trapped in a mountain cabin by a blizzard, stalked by an ancient cannibal demon bent on stealing their sanity—and their lives. (978-1-60282-950-3)

The Blush Factor by Gun Brooke. Ice-cold business tycoon Eleanor Ashcroft only cares about the three Ps—Power, Profit, and Prosperity—until young Addison Garr makes her doubt both that and the state of her frostbitten heart. (978-1-60282-985-5)

Slash and Burn by Valerie Bronwen. The murder of a roundly despised author at an LGBT writers' conference in New Orleans turns Winter Lovelace's relaxing weekend hobnobbing with her peers into a nightmare of suspense—especially when her ex turns up. (978-1-60282-986-2)

The Quickening: A Sisters of Spirits Novel by Yvonne Heidt. Ghosts, visions, and demons are all in a day's work for Tiffany. But when Kat asks for help on a serial killer case, life takes on another dimension altogether. (978-1-60282-975-6)

Smoke and Fire by Julie Cannon. Oil and water, passion and desire, a combustible combination. Can two women fight the fire that draws them together and threatens to keep them apart? (978-1-60282-977-0)

Love and Devotion by Jove Belle. KC Hall trips her way through life, stumbling into an affair with a married bombshell twice her age. Thankfully, her best friend, Emma Reynolds, is there to show her the true meaning of Love and Devotion. (978-1-60282-965-7)

The Shoal of Time by J.M. Redmann. It sounded too easy. Micky Knight is reluctant to take the case because the easy ones often turn into the hard ones, and the hard ones turn into the dangerous ones. In this one, easy turns hard without warning. (978-1-60282-967-1)